LUCY DANIELS

ANIMAL ARK

Puppies in the Pantry

h
**Hodder
Children's
Books**

A division of Hachette Children's Books

Special thanks to Ingrid Hoare
Thanks also to C.J. Hall, B.Vet.Med., M.R.C.V.S., for reviewing
the veterinary information contained in this book.

Animal Ark is a trademark of Working Partners Limited
Text copyright © 1999 Working Partners Limited
Created by Working Partners Limited, London WC1X 9HH
Original series created by Ben M. Baglio
Illustrations copyright © 1999 Ann Baum

Puppies in the Pantry first published in Great Britain in 1994
by Hodder Children's Books

This edition published 2013

The right of Lucy Daniels to be identified as the Author of
the Work has been asserted by her in accordance with the
Copyright, Designs and Patents Act 1988.

1

A Catalogue record for this book is available from the British Library

ISBN 978 1 444 91239 5

Typeset in Baskerville by Avon DataSet Ltd,
Bidford-on-Avon, Warwickshire

Printed and bound by
CPI Group (UK) Ltd, Croydon, CR0 4YY

The paper and board used in this paperback by Hodder Children's Books
are natural recyclable products made from wood grown in sustainable forests.
The manufacturing processes conform to the environmental regulations
of the country of origin.

Hodder Children's Books
a division of Hachette Children's Books
338 Euston Road, London NW1 3BH
An Hachette UK company
www.hachette.co.uk

To Sue Welford

One

'How exciting!' said Mandy's mum, Emily Hope.
'They're going to make a film at Bleakfell Hall.'

Mrs Hope was busily reading the morning's
mail over breakfast. She stuffed the letter back
in its envelope. Breakfast at the Hopes' busy
veterinary practice, Animal Ark, was always a
hurried affair. Fruit juice, cereal, low-fat yoghurt
lately as Mr Hope was on a diet ... toast if you
were lucky. All eaten at a huge old pine table in
their oak-beamed cottage kitchen.

Mandy dragged her eyes away from her last-
minute revision for a biology test that morning.

Mrs Hope took a final mouthful of juice and rose from the table. 'We've been asked to check out the animals they're using,' she said.

Mandy's father looked up from his newspaper. 'Bleakfell Hall, eh? That'll be interesting.' He stroked his dark beard thoughtfully. 'Mixing with the film stars. Don't let it go to your head, Emily!'

Mandy felt a flutter of excitement in her stomach. That would be a real event for the sleepy village of Welford. Famous film stars in their midst! Her friend James Hunter would be excited too, although she knew he really preferred football to films.

'What kind of film are they making, Mum?' Mandy tucked a strand of blonde hair behind her ear. Her blue eyes sparkled. 'One about animals?'

Emily Hope smiled. 'Trust you to think of that, Mandy.' She stood in front of the mirror, ran a comb hurriedly through her long, red hair then tied it back with a green silk scarf. 'Apparently it's a Victorian murder mystery.'

'Wow! Bleakfell Hall's just the place then. I've always thought it kind of spooky. Hear that, Jess?'

Jess, a small Jack Russell terrier, sat at Mandy's feet. Mandy fed her a piece of toast secretly. One huge gulp and it was gone. The terrier gave a little 'woof'.

'Don't think I didn't see that, Mandy.' Mr Hope had a kindly twinkle in his eye. 'She's getting quite podgy. What's Auntie Mary going to say if she comes back from Australia and Jess has put on a stone in weight?'

Mandy giggled. She had been delighted when her Aunt Mary had asked the Hopes to look after Jess for a couple of months while she went to Australia on a university course.

'You know I can't resist those brown eyes, Dad.' Mandy bent to give the little dog an affectionate hug.

'You can't resist any animal that crosses your path,' Mr Hope said.

Mandy grinned. She scratched Jess behind the ear. 'You love toast, don't you, Jess?' Having the terrier to stay at Animal Ark was like heaven to Mandy.

Since turning twelve, Mandy Hope had been allowed to help out at her parents' veterinary practice, Animal Ark, in the pretty Yorkshire village of Welford. Mandy cleaned out cages, helped comfort sick animals . . . nothing was too much trouble. Mandy just couldn't wait to grow up and become a vet herself!

'Well?' Adam Hope looked expectantly at his wife. 'Come on, spill the beans. What animals are they using for the film? Chimps, elephants . . . ?'

'That would be *really* great!' Mandy swallowed her last mouthful of toast and rose from the table.

Dad was teasing of course. Even if it was only cats and dogs Mandy thought it would be brilliant to go and see them. She might even get to see a real film star in the process!

Mrs Hope laughed. 'I don't know exactly. The letter didn't say very much. Just that the animals are being supplied by an agency called Animal Stars and that the company will hire horses from the local stables. They've all got to be vetted before they use them. And . . . oh, yes . . . they mention a dog. Apparently it's one of the stars of the film.'

'What kind of a dog?' Mandy asked.

Her mother shook her head. 'I don't know. Sorry, Mandy.'

'Perhaps it's a mystery dog?' Mandy's

imagination began to run away with her. 'Like in that Sherlock Holmes story: *The Hound of the Baskervilles.*'

Mrs Hope gave her daughter a quick hug. 'You'll just have to be patient, Mandy. They're not coming until Monday.' She dropped a kiss on top of her head. 'As it's half-term you can come up with me if you like.'

'Mum, that would be brilliant!' Mandy exclaimed.

Mrs Hope glanced at the clock. 'Got to rush,' she said. 'Time I opened the surgery.'

Mandy could hear a puppy's excited yelp from the waiting-room of the vet's extension attached to the back of the old stone cottage. She would have loved to go and see the puppy but there was no time. School and the dreaded biology test beckoned.

Mr Hope folded up his newspaper with a sigh. 'Yup, I'd better get going too. I've got to inspect a consignment of beef cattle arriving at Walton market.'

'Time for me to go too.' Mandy gave Jess a last hug. She hated leaving the little terrier shut up in the kitchen while she was at school. If Mandy had her way she would have tucked Jess into her schoolbag and carted her off to lessons. She grabbed her schoolbag. 'I expect James is waiting.'

'No racing to school on that bike of yours,' Mr Hope warned.

'I won't, Dad . . . 'bye, Jess,' Mandy said. 'See you later.'

'And don't slam the door as you go out,' Mr Hope shouted from the sink.

The front door banged loudly as Mandy went out.

The following Monday morning there was a ring at the back door.

'I'll go,' Mandy called from the front room where she had been playing with Jess.

The terrier was ahead of her, hurtling down the corridor like a bullet.

'If it's anyone for me . . .' Mr Hope dodged away from the speeding terrier. He donned his green waxed jacket and tweed cap. '. . . I'm off to Baildon Farm. One of Jack Mabson's cows has got mastitis. I should be back in about an hour.'

'Poor thing,' Mandy muttered. She knew the inflammation of a cow's udder was terribly painful.

'You'd better hurry up then, Dad.'

Mr Hope was checking his bag. 'If it's anyone wanting anything urgent Mum can go after surgery. Or better still, get them to make an appointment with Jean.'

'Yes, Dad.' Mandy almost pushed her father out of the front door. The sooner he got to Baildon and treated that poor cow, the happier Mandy would be.

By now, Jess was hurling herself at the back door with the ferocity of a tiger, and barking furiously. Mandy ran to grab her collar. 'Jess, for goodness' sake, we're not being invaded by aliens.' Mandy scooped the noisy little dog up in her arms.

The antics of the Jack Russell always amused her. She would miss Jess so much when Aunt Mary came back. Mandy had three pet rabbits and she loved them dearly. But they weren't quite as much fun as the little terrier.

Mandy's best friend, James Hunter, stood on the doorstep.

'Oh . . . hi, James.'

James looked cold. The wind ruffled his straight brown hair. Mandy thought he looked a bit like a

Shetland pony but didn't say. She knew James was a bit sensitive and she wouldn't have hurt his feelings for all the world.

Blackie, the Hunters' black Labrador, sat at James's feet. As soon as he saw Jess, Blackie wagged his tail like mad. Jess barked and wriggled furiously. Mandy put her down. The two dogs tore off round the garden, jumping and barking.

Mandy winced. Her dad wouldn't be at all pleased if they crashed through the flower-beds. The two dogs had been great friends from the first moment Jess had come to stay at Animal Ark.

'Blackie!' James called. 'Come here!' The Labrador ignored him, belting round the garden after the agile terrier. James sighed. 'That dog never listens. *Blackie!*' Blackie gave one last excited bark and ran to sit at James's feet. He looked up at James as if to say 'sorry'.

James adjusted his glasses on the bridge of his nose. 'I thought you might want to go for a walk, Mandy,' he said.

'Oh, James, I'm sorry,' said Mandy. 'I'm going out with Mum when surgery's finished.'

James raised his eyebrows. 'Anywhere nice?'

'To Bleakfell Hall. Remember, I told you last

Friday, James. The film.'

James clapped his hand to his forehead. 'Of course you did . . . how stupid. Sorry, Mandy, I forgot.'

'We'll be back later. I'll give you a ring. We could go out then.'

'OK,' James said. 'Come on, Blackie. We'll have to go on our own this morning.' He made a face. 'Looks like I'll have to do that shopping for Mum after all.'

Mandy smiled. She knew James hated going shopping. He would rather be playing with his computer or helping Mandy at Animal Ark.

'If we have to go to Bleakfell Hall again, James, I'll ask Mum if you could come if you like.'

James grinned. 'That would be great. I'd love to.' He waved. 'See you later, Mandy.'

Jess was digging a hole in the flower-bed. Blackie had run off and stood watching.

Mandy whistled. 'Jess, Dad'll go bonkers if you dig up any more of his plants!'

James waved again as he clipped on Blackie's lead and headed off towards the village green.

Mandy felt a bit guilty. James had looked a little downhearted. She sighed. She'd buy him an ice cream later to make up for it. And, with a bit of luck, next time they had to go, James could come too.

Half an hour later Mrs Hope's four-wheel drive vehicle wound its way up the narrow road to Bleakfell Hall. The sun was warm on the windscreen. Crossing the river bridge, Mandy could see its rays hitting the water in a shower of silver sparks. She stared out of the window. The jigsaw pattern of green fields and dry-stone walls flashed past. Mandy opened the window and took a deep breath of fresh moorland air. Her heart drummed with excitement. Visiting film stars was definitely a great way to spend the first day of the half-term!

They turned a corner and the hundred-year-old Bleakfell Hall loomed at the end of its long gravel drive. Its towers and turrets really did look like something out of a murder mystery story.

'I said it looked spooky.' Mandy peered up at the grey-stone house.

Several cars and two huge trailers were parked by the stable block. One of the trailers had 'Curtis-Smith Films Limited' written on the side in black letters.

They drew up outside the dark oak-panelled front door.

'Doesn't Mrs Ponsonby live here any more?' Mandy asked. Mrs Ponsonby was one of the bossiest women in town, and definitely a force to be reckoned with.

'Yes, I saw her in the post office on Saturday morning,' Mandy's mum confirmed. 'But she's gone to stay with her sister while they're using the house. The film company pay loads of money apparently.'

Mandy's eyes lit up. 'Hey,' she said thoughtfully. 'How about offering them an old stone cottage with a vet's surgery attached? Then we could get lots of money too!'

'Mandy!' Her mother laughed. 'You should be ashamed.'

'Not at all,' Mandy said. 'We could give it to the animal sanctuary.' Mandy's heart lurched with pity when she thought about all the wretched and abandoned animals the sanctuary took in.

Mrs Hope smiled at her daughter. 'Mrs Ponsonby really needs the money too. Some of the old house is almost falling down apparently.'

'Oh. I hope it doesn't collapse while they're filming.' Mandy took a wary look at the massive chimneys.

'I wouldn't think so, Mandy. Come on. We'd better find out who's in charge.'

'It'll be great having film stars staying near the village,' Mandy said as she got out. 'I might get their autographs. The girls at school would be really envious.' She looked round. 'I wonder where the animals are?'

'Let's find out.' Mrs Hope took her vet's bag from the car.

They went up the flight of elegant stone steps that led to the front door. Mrs Hope pressed the old-fashioned bell push.

Mandy's heart thudded with excitement as she heard light footsteps coming towards the door. It swung open. A blonde-haired young man in jeans and a college sweatshirt stood in the doorway. He held a clipboard in his hand.

'Good morning,' said Mrs Hope. 'I'm Emily Hope, the vet. I've been asked to take a look at the animals. I hope it's convenient.'

The young man grinned. Behind him, Mandy could see three or four people with ladders. They seemed to be setting up huge lights in the hallway.

'Hi,' the young man said. 'I'm Ben Burton, Mr Curtis's personal assistant. Mr Curtis is the film's director.'

'This is my daughter, Mandy.'

Mandy smiled, feeling shy. It wasn't every day she got to meet a film director's assistant!

'You'll find Mr Baggins and the others in the back kitchen,' Ben explained, stepping back for them to enter.

Mandy gulped. 'Mr Baggins. Who's he?'

Ben's eyes twinkled. 'You'd better go and see.'

Inside, the house seemed to echo with

hammering and banging. From the top of the wide, winding staircase Mandy heard a woman shouting something. The whole place was buzzing.

Suddenly a head appeared over the first floor banister. 'Ben, Mr Curtis wants you – *now*!' a young woman with a white scarf tied round her head and red dangly earrings shouted down.

'Oh, dear.' Ben looked slightly flustered. 'He'll go spare if I don't go at once. Go through into the kitchen, Mrs Hope, Mandy. Someone there will help you.' He ran his hand through his hair. 'To be honest, I'm not sure about anything at the moment. Must go!' He ran up the staircase two steps at a time.

'But . . .' Mrs Hope looked at her daughter and shrugged. 'Oh, well,' she said. 'Let's see if we can find the kitchen and Mr Baggins, whoever he might be!'

'Perhaps he's the man in charge of the animals. Funny name though,' Mandy added.

Crossing the hall seemed a bit dangerous. There were thick cables absolutely everywhere on the floor. Ladders trembled overhead. Workmen with hammers in their belts scurried around like ants.

'It's like that assault course at the adventure centre,' Mandy remarked, hopping over a thick cable that snaked across the floor.

'I think this is it.' Mrs Hope pushed open a large oak door. 'I've been here once before when Mrs Ponsonby's Pekinese was sick.'

The door led them through into a dark, oak-panelled corridor. Another door at the end was ajar. From inside a voice screeched.

'She loves you yeah, yeah, yeah! She loves you yeah, yeah, yeah! A cup of tea with two sugars, cup of tea with two sugars!'

Mandy's mum turned to look at her. They both giggled.

'I bet I know who that is!' Mandy skipped on ahead. She couldn't wait to see the owner of that strange voice.

Two

Mandy pushed open the door. She had guessed the voice came from a parrot. And there it was, sitting on the edge of the table in the huge Victorian kitchen. Beady, black eyes stared at her.

'Oh!' Mandy breathed. 'Mum, he's gorgeous!'

She stepped forward and stretched out her hand to stroke the bright red and green feathers.

'This has got to be Mr Baggins,' Mandy said. The bird arched its neck in response to Mandy's gentle caress.

'*Two cups of tea and a sugar,*' it murmured in a funny, soft voice. Mandy loved the feel of his feathers against her fingertips. Scratchy, yet soft at the same time.

'Who's a lovely boy, then?' she said softly.

A *thump, thump* came from over by the fire. Curled up on the seat was a beautiful black Labrador. Its long, silky tail beat a welcome to Mandy and Mrs Hope.

'Hello, old girl.' Mrs Hope crouched down to stroke the dog. 'Her name's Charley,' she said, examining the disc on the dog's red collar.

'She's beautiful,' Mandy said, stroking behind Charley's ears. 'I bet she's the star of the film.'

There was more. Three sleek cats were curled on the fireside rug. One purred gently, its pink nose turned upwards. All had soft, red collars with silver discs.

'This one's Snowy . . .' Mandy looked at the disc, '. . . and this one's Echo. What lovely names.' Echo, a small tabby cat, stirred and stretched lazily under Mandy's loving fingers.

'What's the grey one called?' Mrs Hope asked.

'Sky. These must be the "others" Ben told us about.'

'I guess so.' Mrs Hope looked round. 'I wonder who's in charge of them.'

Just then a tall, burly man came in through the back door. He wiped his boots on the mat. Mandy heard him sniff, then snort. He was wearing a green quilted jacket and a flat cap. His ears stuck out like jug handles and he had a rough, red face.

Charley jumped off the chair. She eyed the man suspiciously and sat down on the floor beside Mandy, pressing herself against Mandy's legs. Mandy had a strange feeling. It was as if Charley had suddenly decided Mandy was her owner – as if she wanted Mandy to look after and protect her. Mandy put her hand down and let it rest softly on Charley's sleek head. A small whine came from the Labrador's throat.

'It's OK, Charley,' Mandy whispered. 'I'll look after you, don't worry. There's no need to be nervous.' But it was clear at once to Mandy that Charley wasn't at all fond of the man who had just come into the kitchen.

'Good morning,' the man said in a deep, gravelly voice.

'Good morning.' Mrs Hope held out her hand.

'I'm Emily Hope, the vet. This is my daughter, Mandy.'

The man shook Mrs Hope's hand and nodded to Mandy. 'George Sims,' he said gruffly.

'Perhaps you can help, George,' Mrs Hope went on. 'We're looking for the person in charge of these animals.'

Mr Sims tipped his cap to the back of his head. 'It looks like I am,' he muttered.

Mrs Hope frowned. 'I don't understand.'

He pulled out a chair and sat down. Charley was still sitting against Mandy's legs. She felt the dog jump nervously at the sound of the chair legs scraping on the flagstone floor.

'There's been a bit of a problem,' Mr Sims explained. 'I do work for Animal Stars but I'm really only the driver. The girl who's supposed to supervise the animals hasn't turned up.'

'What's happened to her?' Mrs Hope asked.

Mr Sims shrugged. 'Not really sure – some mix-up about locations. She's gone off to France to do a commercial for pet food when she should be here with this lot.'

'Oh, dear,' said Mrs Hope.

'They've asked me to stay until she turns up,'

Mr Sims went on grumpily. 'I mean what do I know about looking after a parrot?'

Mr Baggins squawked, '*Mr Sugar, cup of bags.*'

Mandy giggled, then put her hand over her mouth.

'Well,' Mrs Hope said, 'I'm sure we could give you any advice you need. Especially if its only for a day or so. I'm sure the agency will send someone as soon as possible.'

'I jolly well hope so,' Mr Sims said, still looking grumpy.

Snowy, the white cat, got up from his place by the fire. Purring, he rubbed himself against Mr Sims's corduroy trousers, arching his back and waving his tail like a flag.

Mr Sims moved his legs away. Mandy stepped forward and picked Snowy up, cradling him in her arms.

'Can't stand cats,' George Sims muttered. He glared at Mr Baggins. 'Nor parrots.'

Mr Baggins stared back at him with beady eyes.

'*Left, right, left, right, quick march!*' Mr Baggins suddenly screeched.

Mandy put her hand over her mouth to stop

herself from bursting into laughter.

'Bah!' said Mr Sims.

Mandy bit her lip, suddenly feeling serious. How on earth could anyone dislike either Snowy or Mr Baggins? Both of them were beautiful and perfectly harmless.

'Right,' Mrs Hope went on in a businesslike way. 'My job is to examine the animals. Shall I do it here?'

George Sims shrugged. 'If you like.'

Charley suddenly got up and ran through a door beside the old pine dresser.

'Charley!' Mandy called. 'Where's she going?' she asked Mr Sims.

'She's made her bed in the pantry,' Mr Sims said. 'Best place for her. Keeps her out of the way until she's needed.'

Mandy felt sorry for the Labrador, hiding away in a cold pantry when a cosy fire burned in the hearth.

'Who shall I give the certificate to?' Mrs Hope was asking.

'Certificate?' Mr Sims looked blank.

'Yes, I have to pass the animals as fit before the film company can use them.'

'Leave it on the table if you like. I'll pick it up after my break.'

Mandy was trying to persuade Charley to come out of the pantry.

'Come on, Charley. Mum wants to have a look at you.'

'I should leave her,' Mr Sims said, opening the back door. 'She's a bit moody if you ask me.'

'Well, she is an actor,' Mandy said. She thought George Sims might feel moody too if he was being looked after by someone who didn't much like him.

Mr Sims snorted. He went out and slammed the door behind him.

'He's not very keen on animals, is he, Mum?' Mandy said. She coaxed the Labrador out of the pantry. 'Come on, Charley, Mum won't hurt you.'

'I think he's just a bit worried,' Mrs Hope replied. 'He's had the job rather thrust upon him by the looks of it. Let's hope the proper trainer arrives soon.'

Mandy sat on the floor with her arms round the Labrador's neck. She rubbed her cheek against the shining coat. Her heart stirred. If George Sims just took time to get to know Charley he'd soon find out how gorgeous she was.

'Come on, Charley.' Mrs Hope lifted the big dog on to the table. 'Let's have a look at you then.'

She examined the dog gently. Ears . . . eyes . . . teeth. All looked fine. She felt Charley's sleek, muscled back and ran her hands over her legs. She held Charley's head between her hands and looked at her muzzle. Then she ruffled the hair on the back of Charley's head and lifted her down.

'She's great,' Mrs Hope said. 'A picture of health.'

'Are you going to look at Mr Baggins?' Mandy asked when her mum had finished examining the three cats.

'*Mr Baggins . . . Mr Baggins!*' the parrot suddenly screeched. '*A cup of tea and two Baggins.*'

Mandy burst out laughing. Mrs Hope laughed too. 'Yes, but I'm almost certain there's nothing wrong with him,' she said.

Mrs Hope carefully wrapped the bird in a tea towel and gently examined him. She stroked the parrot's feathers and put him back on the table. 'His claws look a bit long but nothing to worry about.'

Suddenly Mr Baggins took off, flying up and landing on one of the high oak beams of the ceiling.

'I wonder what part he plays in the film?' Mandy asked.

'A naughty part, I should think.' Mrs Hope took a book from her bag. She sat at the table and wrote something on one of the pages. 'I think I'd better wait to explain these certificates to George.'

'Do you think it's OK if I take a look round the house?' Mandy asked. 'I'd love to see the film set.'

'I should think so. Don't get in anyone's way, though. It looked pretty chaotic out there.'

'I'll take Charley,' Mandy spied a dog lead hanging from a hook on the back door.

'And don't be too long,' Mrs Hope added. 'I've got to call on Mrs Platt on the way back.'

Mandy's heart skipped a beat. She knew Mrs Platt's poodle had been ill for a long time. 'Not Brandy again?' she said anxiously.

Mrs Hope looked grim. 'Yes, I'm afraid so. Mrs Platt rang this morning and asked me to call in to look at him.'

'Oh, dear.' Mandy's heart sank. Brandy, Mrs Platt's poodle, was very old and had trouble with his kidneys. Mandy had a horrible feeling that this time there wouldn't be any pills that would make him better.

Mrs Hope patted Mandy's arm. 'Cheer up, Mandy. It may not be as bad as you think.'

'I hope not,' Mandy said. 'I don't know what Mrs Platt will do without a dog. She'll be really lonely.'

Mrs Platt's husband had died over a year ago. Since then, Brandy had been her only companion.

She had a son but he lived miles away in London and couldn't visit very often.

Mandy pulled herself together. There was no use worrying about it. Whatever happened, neither Mrs Platt nor her mum would want poor Brandy to suffer.

'Come on, Charley,' she said. 'Let's see if we can spot any film stars out there.'

In the hall, a single huge spotlight was being erected in the corner. A short, balding man with an extremely large stomach and a loud voice to match was shouting instructions. He wore an out-of-shape grey T-shirt that announced he was 'The Boss'.

'No – point it this way!' he yelled. 'We want it to look as if the light's coming through the window, not from a hole in the ceiling!'

'Hello, young lady.' The man had spotted Mandy. 'Are you the animal trainer?'

'Er – no,' Mandy stammered. 'I'm Mandy Hope, the vet's daughter. I'm just taking Charley for a little look round.'

The man bent down to pat Charley affectionately. Mandy could see he liked dogs. She always knew when people were good with animals. And, as far as Mandy was concerned, anyone who liked animals had got to be a nice person.

'Is Charley the star?' Mandy asked.

'She surely is.' The man looked over his shoulder. 'But don't tell Antonia that.'

'Antonia?'

'Miss Antonia Kent. Our *human* star.'

Mandy giggled.

'The dog sees it all happen.'

'Gosh!' Mandy's eyes were wide. 'Sees what . . . not the murder?'

The man looked sombre. 'Yes, the dirty deed itself. The lady of the manor stabs her husband in a fit of jealousy in this very hallway. Her pet dog – she's called Black Rose in the story – witnesses the terrible crime.'

Mandy was staring at him, wide-eyed. 'Wow!' She felt quite breathless.

'Why don't you stay to watch the filming?' the man said. 'Maybe Charley will give a truly great performance if you're here. You two certainly look as if you're great friends already.'

'We are.' Mandy grinned. She felt pleased the man had noticed how well she and Charley were getting along. She patted Charley's head affectionately. 'I'd love to stay and watch.' Then she remembered something important she had to do. Her face fell. 'Oh . . . but I can't. I'm sorry. I've got to go back with my mum.'

Mandy would love to have stayed with Charley. But she had to see Mrs Platt's dear little Brandy. And if he was so ill that nothing could be done to cure him then Mrs Platt might well need a shoulder to cry on.

Just then, Ben came running down the stairs.

'There you are, Mr Curtis!'

'Mr Curtis!' Mandy gasped. She hadn't realised the man really was 'The Boss'!

'I've been looking all over for you,' Ben went on. 'Miss Kent's throwing a tantrum again.'

The sound of crashing china came from one of the upstairs rooms. *Oh dear,* Mandy thought. *That's not all she's throwing.*

Mr Curtis sighed heavily. 'What now, Ben?'

'She says she won't work with a parrot. She says she's allergic to birds and that it might have fleas or something.'

'Fleas!' Mandy couldn't help blurting out. 'Mr Baggins has got nothing of the sort.'

Mr Curtis sighed again. He turned to Mandy. 'These actresses are so temperamental. I'd better go and calm her down. Ben, look after this young lady, will you?'

Just then, Mrs Hope came through from the kitchen. Charley wagged her tail in greeting.

'Mum,' Mandy said. 'This is Mr Curtis, the film's director.'

Mrs Hope shook his hand. 'The animals are all fine,' she said. 'You can begin using them whenever you're ready.' She handed him the certificate. 'I was going to give this to George Sims but I can't wait any longer.'

Mandy saw Ben and Mr Curtis exchange worried glances.

'I'm afraid he's not turning out to be very reliable,' Ben said with a frown. 'Let's hope the proper trainer turns up soon.'

'Yes,' Mrs Hope agreed. 'Let's hope so.'

Mr Curtis strode off up the stairs.

Ben took Charley's lead from Mandy's hand and ushered them to the front door.

'Could I bring my friend James next time?' asked Mandy. 'He's mad about animals.'

'I don't see why not,' Ben replied. 'And as

George doesn't seem to have much idea what to do with them, it looks as if we might be very glad of your help!'

Three

'I'm a bit worried about Charley,' Mandy said as they drove back down into Welford. They went along the upper high street, past the church, past the Old School House adult education centre that used to be the village school until a few years ago. They soon reached the estate of modern bungalows where Mrs Platt lived with Brandy.

'Why?' Mandy's mother glanced in her direction.

'She just doesn't seem very happy.' Mandy had

been worrying about Charley ever since they left the hall. 'A dog needs love and affection, not a smelly old blanket on the floor of a cold pantry.'

Mrs Hope patted her daughter's knee. 'She's OK, Mandy. She's just taking a little time to settle down. Remember how Jess was when she first came to stay with us?'

Mandy managed a small smile. 'Yes,' she said. 'I think she missed her boyfriend.'

'Who, Tad?' Tad was the Jack Russell that lived next door to Aunt Mary. Mrs Hope laughed. 'Yes, I expect you're right, Mandy. And don't worry about Charley. We'll keep a good eye on her.'

Mandy felt reassured. Her mother was always right.

They drew up outside a semi-detached bungalow with a large back garden at the end of the row. They got out and went round past rows of neatly planted vegetables to the back door.

Mrs Platt hurried to answer their knock.

'Thank goodness you're here,' she said anxiously. 'I was afraid I'd missed you. I just had to pop along to the church to renew the water in the vases.' Mrs Platt was well known in the village for her floral arrangements. 'Come in, come in.'

The bungalow kitchen was warm and cosy. Pots and pans shone on the shelves and bright red and blue curtains adorned the windows.

'I've kept the radiator on for poor Brandy,' Mrs Platt explained. 'I thought he might feel better if he was tucked up nice and warm.' Her voice trembled a little. Mandy felt really sorry for Mrs Platt.

Brandy, a miniature champagne poodle, lay in his basket. Mandy felt her throat swell and her eyes began to fill with tears. The little dog's eyes were red and weepy, and his coat looked dull. 'Poor Brandy,' she whispered. She remembered Brandy when he was bright and active, a dear, friendly little animal. She crouched down beside the basket.

Mrs Hope gently probed the dog's swollen stomach. Her fingers touched a tender spot and the poodle gave a little whine. Mandy winced. She wished she could take the dog's pain away.

Mrs Hope rose. Her face looked sad. 'I'm sorry, Mrs Platt. If those tablets I gave him last week haven't worked . . .'

Mrs Platt shook her head. 'He did seem a bit

better. We even went for a little walk yesterday
when I got in from church. But this morning he
wouldn't even get out of his basket. I had to carry
him out to do his business.'

Mandy stroked Brandy's curly coat. The little
dog felt hot, and his nose was dry. She felt a tear
creep from beneath her eyelid and trickle down
her cheek. It fell on Brandy's fur.

'He's in a good deal of pain, I'm afraid,' Mrs
Hope was saying. 'I really think the kindest thing
would be to put him to sleep.'

Mandy looked up through a mist of tears. Mrs
Hope had her arm round Mrs Platt's shoulders.

'Yes,' Mrs Platt nodded. 'You're right, of course.
We can't let him suffer. If you're absolutely
sure . . . ?'

Mrs Hope nodded sadly. 'I can give him an
injection now, or you could bring him along to
the surgery.'

'No . . . no.' Mrs Platt took a hanky from her
trouser pocket and blew her nose loudly. 'Brandy
would want to go to sleep in his own basket.'

Mrs Hope opened her bag and took out a
syringe.

Mandy wiped her eyes with the back of her

hand. She drew in a deep breath. It really was no good crying. All the tears in the world wouldn't make Brandy better. She tried to pull herself together. 'Would you like me to help you, Mum?'

'No, it's all right, thanks. Why don't you take Mrs Platt into the garden? Take a look at those lovely roses. Unless you want to stay?'

Mrs Platt shook her head. 'No. I'm not very good at this sort of thing.' She knelt down by Brandy's basket. The little dog lifted his head at the sight of his mistress. Mrs Platt stroked his head gently. Mandy could see she was crying.

Mrs Platt bent and touched Brandy's head with her lips. Mandy put a hand out to steady her as she rose to her feet.

'Come on, Mrs Platt. Let's see those roses.'

Mandy shut the door gently behind them. She swallowed the tears that threatened to spill over once again. There seemed to be a hard lump in her throat.

She linked her arm through Mrs Platt's as they walked slowly up the garden path. Mrs Platt blew her nose once then seemed to recover.

'There's no use crying,' she said in a determined voice. 'Brandy has had a wonderful life. He's been treated like a little prince. It's wrong to let him suffer.'

Mandy managed a sad little smile. 'Yes.' Mrs Platt was right, of course, but it was still horrible to think they would never see Brandy alive again.

'See this . . .' Mrs Platt pointed to a pink climbing rose just coming into flower. 'I brought this with me from my old house. My husband gave it to me for my birthday – the same birthday my son gave Brandy to me.' She sighed. 'What a gorgeous little puppy Brandy was. Nothing but a bundle of fluff with two huge black eyes—'

Her voice broke. 'He's twelve years old you know, Mandy.'

'Same age as me,' Mandy said softly. They looked at each other and smiled. There was a bond of understanding between them. Dear little Brandy wouldn't be running up the garden any more but at least Mrs Platt had this beautiful rose to remember him by.

'Will you get another dog?' Mandy asked as they reached the end of the garden and looked out towards the high moors. She felt a bit better. It was time to think about the future and not the past.

Mrs Platt shook her head. 'I'm afraid I can't afford one. I don't earn much with my little job at the grocer's shop.'

Mandy turned to see her mother standing by the back door drying her hands on a towel. They walked back towards her.

'How . . . ?' Mrs Platt began. Mandy heard a tremble in her voice.

'He just went to sleep peacefully,' Mrs Hope assured her.

Mandy squeezed Mrs Platt's arm.

'What would you like me to do with Brandy,

now, Mrs Platt?' Mrs Hope asked gently. 'I've wrapped him in his blanket.'

Mandy looked past her mum and Mrs Platt. She could just see a pathetic little bundle wrapped in a blue blanket lying in Brandy's basket. She felt the tears coming again but managed to hold them back.

'I'll see to him, don't worry,' replied Mrs Platt. 'I'll bury him beneath the rose. 'He'll like it there. It was his favourite place on a hot summer's day. Nice and shady, you see.'

Mandy could just imagine Brandy as he used to be, and she knew they had done the right thing.

'How much do I owe you, Emily?' Mrs Platt said in a practical voice. She squared her shoulders. Mandy admired her bravery. She didn't think she would ever get used to animals having to die this way.

'Don't worry about that. I'll get Jean to send the bill at the end of the month.'

Mandy gave Mrs Platt a hug. 'I hope you won't be too lonely.'

Mrs Platt managed a wan smile. 'Maybe I'll get a budgie. They're not so expensive to keep.'

'No, but you can't take a budgie for a walk,' Mandy said sadly.

Mrs Platt watched from the window as they drove away. Mandy thought she looked so lonely with no little dog to cuddle in her arms.

They headed straight back to Animal Ark. The village high street was quiet.

Mrs Hope patted her daughter's knee. 'Cheer up, Mandy.'

'I'm trying to,' Mandy said. 'I just know how Mrs Platt will miss poor Brandy.'

'I know, darling.'

Mandy looked thoughtful. 'You know, Mum, Mrs Platt would really love another poodle. She just can't afford one.'

'They are pretty expensive.' Mrs Hope changed gear to go round the sharp bend.

'I know. That's what she said. I've been thinking . . .'

'What?' Mrs Hope glanced knowingly at her daughter. 'What scheme are you cooking up now, Mandy?'

'I just thought maybe they'd have one at the animal sanctuary.'

'Yes, they might.' Mrs Hope raised her eyebrows.

Mandy jiggled about in her seat. 'Could we go up there now?'

'Hang on a minute, Mandy. Give Mrs Platt time to get over poor old Brandy.'

'But having a new pet will help her,' Mandy insisted. Once Mandy had an idea in her head, wild horses wouldn't drag it away.

'We'll go as soon as your dad or I have a spare minute. Does that suit you?'

Mandy sighed. 'Yes, OK, but you won't forget, will you?'

'I don't suppose you'll let me!'

They pulled up under the wooden sign that said 'Animal Ark, Veterinary Surgeon'.

Mandy jumped out, anxious to see Jess. She felt better now. The thought of finding a new dog for Mrs Platt had cheered her up no end.

'I'll just check with Jean to see if there's been any calls.' Mrs Hope headed for the surgery door.

Mandy hurried through into the kitchen. Jess was curled up in her basket, fast asleep. She hadn't even heard the door open.

'Jess!'

The little dog opened her eyes sleepily as Mandy bent to cuddle her.

'Jess,' Mandy said again. 'You lazy old thing. You didn't even hear me come in. You're getting to be a real lazybones.'

Jess licked her face. Mandy picked her up and gave her a quick cuddle.

Mandy went to the phone and dialled James's number. He answered after a dozen rings.

'Oh . . .' Mandy said. 'I was just about to give up.'

'Sorry,' James said. 'I was playing with my new computer game.'

Mandy screwed up her nose. She hated computer games. 'Do you still want to come over later?' she asked.

'You bet. How did you get on at Bleakfell Hall?'

'It was great. I'll tell you all about it when you get here.'

After lunch, Mandy helped Simon, Animal Ark's nurse, with his jobs at the back of the surgery. Simon was laying newspapers on the bottom of one of the animal cages. Mandy was washing and drying the feed bowls.

'Simon?' Mandy said. 'Any idea if the animal

sanctuary would have a poodle for Mrs Platt?'

Simon, a young man in his twenties, tall and thin with fair hair, shrugged his shoulders. 'I don't know, Mandy. I know they get all sorts of dogs handed in.'

Mandy breathed a sigh. 'Aren't people horrible?' she said, suddenly feeling angry as she always did at the thought of all the abandoned and unwanted animals at the sanctuary.

Simon gave a little smile. '*Some* people are, Mandy. Not everyone.'

'You know what I mean.' Mandy thought of Simon as a good friend. Someone to talk things over with if her mum and dad were a bit too busy to listen straight away.

'I mean people who abandon animals,' Mandy went on, still feeling angry. 'Remember that cat I found? Walton. We thought someone had abandoned her because she was pregnant. I was so angry. Why don't people realise a pet is for life, not something you can throw away like . . . like . . .' Mandy felt so indignant all of a sudden she couldn't think of the right word.

'Like an empty cornflake box?' Simon suggested.

'Exactly,' Mandy said.

'You know it's not always people's own fault.' Simon tried to calm her down. 'Sometimes people move house and can't take their pet . . . sometimes they just can't cope with them any longer.'

'Yes, I suppose so,' Mandy agreed. 'But people *should* be more responsible.'

'Can't argue with that,' Simon said with a grin.

Mandy stacked the feed bowls inside one another and put the damp tea towel in the dirty linen basket. She looked at her watch. 'Is there anything else I can do to help, Simon? James should be here in a minute. We're taking the dogs for a walk.'

'No, thanks, Mandy.' Simon was washing his hands. 'That's great.'

Just then James arrived. He handed Mandy a packet of sherbet. 'I got you this at the shop,' he said, grinning. 'I know it's your favourite.'

Mandy was going to hug him then thought he might be embarrassed in front of Simon. 'Thanks, James,' she said. 'Come on. I'll tell you all about Charley, the film star dog.'

Four

The next morning Mandy jumped out of bed. The garden sparkled in the morning sun. There had been a storm in the night. Mandy had woken once to a tremendous crack of thunder.

She had a tight knot of excitement in her stomach. With a bit of luck George Sims would ring from Bleakfell Hall today to say the horses had arrived. She would get to see Charley and Mr Baggins again!

But when the telephone rang it was Grandad.

'Will you be coming to see us during the holiday, Mandy?' he asked as she picked up the receiver.

Mandy smiled. She loved visiting her grandparents at Lilac Cottage, just up the lane from Animal Ark.

'Yes, 'course, Grandad. I'm hoping to go out with Mum this morning, but James and I could come over later if you like.'

'Oh, good. Your Gran's trying out this new recipe for chocolate orange cake and she thought you might like to try it,' Grandad said.

'Yum,' said Mandy. 'We'll definitely be over later, Grandad.'

Mandy felt a bit restless. She'd got her chores to do in the surgery but couldn't seem to settle down to anything. Luckily, the call from Bleakfell Hall came just a few minutes later.

'The horses have arrived,' Mrs Hope said, popping her head round the door.

'Great!' Mandy said excitedly, full of energy all of a sudden. 'I'll ring James.'

James arrived on his bike just as they were getting in the car. Mandy could see he had rushed. His tracksuit top was on back to front but she figured she'd wait to tell him.

Jess climbed on to James's lap, curled up and fell asleep straight away.

When they arrived at Bleakfell Hall they could hear a lot of shouting from inside.

They left Jess curled up in the back of the car, making sure to leave the windows open.

'Perhaps we'd better go round to the yard,' Mrs Hope suggested. 'It sounds as if they're pretty busy in there. I know where the stables are.'

'Let's go and find Charley,' Mandy said to James.

There was no answer to their knock on the back door. Cautiously, Mandy opened it and put her head round.

'Hello . . . anybody here?' She turned to James. 'Come on, I'm sure they won't mind if we go in.'

The vast kitchen was empty. No Charley, no Mr Baggins, no cats, no George Sims. Where on earth was everyone?

The sound of Mr Curtis's voice came echoing along the passage that led to the great hallway.

Mandy pulled James's sleeve. 'Come on, let's take a look. Perhaps all the animals are on the set.'

They crept along the corridor and peered round the half-open door.

The place was in an uproar.

Mandy stifled a giggle. 'I told you it was chaotic,' she whispered to James.

Mr Curtis sat on top of a stepladder, waving his arms about. The ladder wobbled. Ben rushed forward to steady it. Mandy put her hand over her mouth to stop the laughter coming out.

'No!' Mr Curtis was shouting. 'Not there – for goodness' sake, someone get hold of that parrot!'

A woman in an ankle-length white frock was sitting by the fireplace. There was a blanket over her head. The cats were asleep on the sofa as if nothing was going on.

'That must be Antonia Kent,' Mandy whispered in James's ear. 'She's the human star.'

'I'm not acting with that beastly bird!' a voice came from under the blanket. 'I'm not, I'm not, I'm not!'

'Look!' Mandy said, suddenly spying the parrot. 'There's Mr Baggins!'

Sure enough, high up on the elegant, crystal chandelier, Mr Baggins preened his feathers.

Beneath, an assistant held up a cup of sunflower seeds.

'Come down, Mr Baggins,' she was shouting. 'Nice dinner.'

'*Two sugars!*' the parrot screeched. '*A cup of Baggins if you please.*'

Mandy was laughing so much she felt sure someone would hear.

'Where's that blasted George Sims?' Mr Curtis yelled suddenly. 'He's supposed to be supervising these wretched creatures.'

'What a mess,' James whispered.

'We'd better get out of here before we get told off,' Mandy said.

But it was too late. They had been spotted.

'Ah, young lady,' Mr Curtis called from his ladder. 'Come in, come in. Any hope of you getting that bird to come down?'

Mandy and James sidled into the hall. Mandy looked up. 'I'll try,' she said. She felt a bit shy in front of all of the crew. 'But I can't promise.'

Across the hall, Antonia Kent peeped out from under her blanket. Mandy almost laughed again. The actress looked like a nun in a dance frock with the white blanket round her face. But when she took the blanket right off, Mandy drew in her breath. She recognised her straight away. Antonia Kent was the heroine of one of Mandy's favourite soap operas! She just couldn't help staring.

'Mandy . . .' James nudged her in the ribs.

'Oh!' Mandy shook herself. She stood under the chandelier. 'Mr Baggins,' she called softly. 'Come on down, Mr Baggins. You're being very naughty.'

'*She loves you yeah, yeah, yeah,*' Mr Baggins said.

'Yes,' Mandy couldn't help grinning. 'I know, but please come down, huh?'

Mandy heard laughter echoing round the set. She glanced at Mr Curtis. He had a face like thunder. He definitely didn't think it was funny even if everyone else did.

Mandy pursed her lips. She pretended to frown. 'Now come on, Mr Baggins, stop mucking about.' Someone passed her the bowl of sunflower seeds and she held them out. 'Come on . . . please.'

To Mandy's relief, Mr Baggins cocked his head on one side, spread his bright wings, and fluttered down towards her. He landed on her head. Mandy tottered. Then she caught sight of herself in a big, gold framed wall mirror. She looked as if she was wearing a gaily coloured hat in an Easter parade. She put her hand up. 'Come on, you rotten thing. You're holding everyone up.'

Mr Baggins stepped daintily on to her fingers. A sigh of relief washed round the room.

'Well *done*, darling.' Antonia Kent swept towards Mandy in a wave of pale silk and strong perfume. She had black hair, tied up in curls on top of her head, and a pale complexion with a dark beauty spot on her rouged cheek. The actress eyed the parrot warily as she put her arm round Mandy's shoulders. 'This girl's got a magic touch.' She turned to the crew. 'Is she the new animal trainer? Has that hopeless man gone at last?'

Mr Curtis wobbled down his ladder. 'No,' he said. 'She's the vet's daughter. That was terrific, Mandy. Maybe you could stay and help out? We need Charley next. Perhaps you'd fetch her?'

'Oh, yes,' Mandy's heart leapt with excitement. 'I'd love to.'

Just then the front door opened and George Sims came through into the hall. He looked upset. His green wellies were covered with mud. His face was red, as if he had been running.

'Ah, Sims,' Mr Curtis said, 'I was just sending Mandy to fetch the dog.'

George Sims bit his lip. 'The dog's gone,' he said gruffly, looking down at the toes of his boots. 'Run off.'

'What!' Mr Curtis groaned.

Mandy's stomach turned icy with fear. 'Oh, no!' she cried. 'When?'

George Sims looked at her. His face was full of remorse. 'I put her out last night and she didn't come back in. The thunder – it must have scared her.'

A tide of anger and fear washed over Mandy. How could anyone be so daft? 'You put her out during a storm? Don't you know dogs hate thunder?' she exploded.

Mr Sims pursed his lips. 'I didn't know, did I? I told you I'm only the driver. Anyway, she seemed to have settled down. I thought she'd be OK.'

Mandy whirled round. 'Come on, James, we'd better go and look for her.'

'If the dog's been gone all night,' Ben said, 'she could be anywhere.'

'I've been out there looking.' George Sims took

off his cap and scratched his head. 'She's gone, that's for sure.'

'Well, we're going to look anyway.' Mandy's eyes blazed. She and James dashed from the hall.

'Where shall we start?' James panted behind her.

'We'll get Jess. She's good at sniffing scents.'

'But she's never met Charley.'

Mandy was already opening the tail-gate of the car. 'Come on, Jess.' She clipped on the terrier's lead. 'We'll let her sniff Charley's blanket. That might do the trick.'

They ran round the back and into the kitchen. 'Look, Jess.' Mandy thrust open the pantry door. Jess ran inside. She sniffed Charley's blanket and made a little whine in her throat. She began scratching it up to make a bed.

'No, Jess!' Mandy pulled the lead gently. 'No time to sleep now. Charley is missing and we've got to find her!'

'We'd better tell your mum,' James said.

They dashed out into the yard. In the stable, Mrs Hope was examining a beautiful bay gelding. 'What on earth's happened?' Mrs Hope asked in surprise.

'It's Charley,' Mandy blurted. 'She's run off.'

'Run off . . . oh, dear. When?'

'Last night.' Mandy's voice broke. The thought of the beautiful Labrador lost on the moors was awful.

'Mr Sims let her out during the storm,' James explained. 'She must have been really scared. He's been looking for her all morning.'

'We're taking Jess to look for her,' Mandy said.

'It might be an idea to search the outbuildings,' Mrs Hope said. 'She could be hiding.'

'Good thinking,' Mandy said. 'Come on, James. Let's go.'

'Mandy, don't go far. I've got to get back to the surgery and don't forget you promised to visit Gran and Grandad.'

'But we can't just leave . . .'

'I'm sorry, Mandy. Look, there's all the crew to look for her.' Mrs Hope put her arm round Mandy's shoulders. 'I'm sure they'll find her. Just do what you can while you're here. OK?'

Mandy sniffed, then nodded. 'OK, Mum. Come on, James. Let's go.'

* * *

By the time Mrs Hope was ready to leave, the outbuildings had been thoroughly combed for signs of the missing dog.

'Charley! Charley!' They had looked all over. The stables, the hay loft, the old dairy. Mandy and James and Jess had run round the grounds, peering in the shrubbery, the old walled kitchen garden, the tool-shed. They had even gone up into the attic of Bleakfell Hall. But Charley was nowhere to be seen. Eventually it was time to get back.

As they drove down the road, Mandy felt miserable. What had promised to be such a great day had turned out to be just rotten.

'Cheer up, Mandy.' Her mother put a reassuring hand on Mandy's knee. 'You've done all you can to find Charley. The dog is really the film company's responsibility, not ours.'

'I know,' said Mandy. 'But I *told* Charley I'd look after her. I can't let her down.'

In the back of the car James sat silently hugging the tired terrier. It seemed as if they had run for miles in their hunt for the missing dog, and they were both exhausted.

'We haven't really done *anything*,' Mandy

suddenly felt angry. She looked at her mother. 'All we've done is searched some silly old buildings and garden. Charley could be miles away by now and we're doing nothing to help.'

'You'll have to be content with that for now, Mandy,' Mrs Hope said firmly. 'We're going up to Syke Farm. I rang Jean from Bleakfell Hall to see if there were any messages. Mrs Janeki wants me to look at a ewe that's been injured. If you keep a lookout, you might see Charley.'

Mandy sighed. She gazed out of the window. She just wished they hadn't had to leave when they did.

Ahead, the moors and dales seemed to stretch endlessly into the distance. The thought of Charley out there somewhere, lonely and lost, was almost too much to bear. Charley could be lying injured at the bottom of a high rock, shivering with wet and cold . . . hungry. Mandy couldn't stop the rush of terrible thoughts.

'We could ask around the village when we get back,' James said in a small voice. 'Someone might have seen Charley.'

'Yes, you're right, James,' Mandy said, her head clearing. She realised there was lots they could do. 'We could put posters up,' she said, brightening.

'You see,' Mrs Hope said, changing gear to turn into Syke Farm. 'You've only just begun to help.'

Mandy felt a lot better as the car pulled into the farmyard. It was certainly no use moping about. You had to think positive. And thinking positive meant doing everything they could to find Charley!

In the farmyard, Mr Janeki stood in the doorway of the barn. He wore brown overalls and black, muddy wellingtons. His round face looked grim.

'Better stay in the car, you two,' Mrs Hope said, getting out. 'I shan't be long.'

Mandy saw the farmer greet Mrs Hope. They stood talking. Mr Janeki pointed his finger towards the field that bordered the farmyard. Then he and Mrs Hope disappeared into the barn.

Mandy turned to James. 'We'll tell Gran and Grandad about Charley,' she said. 'They'll have some ideas. Gran's always a help if you're in trouble. And Grandad might take us out in his camper to search the dales.'

'Great idea.' James brightened up. 'And I'll do all I can to help.'

'Thanks, James,' Mandy said with a sigh. It was great to have such a good friend, she thought.

Mrs Hope came out of the barn with Mr Janeki. Her face was grave as she came towards the car and got in.

'What's up, Mum?' Mandy asked.

'One of Mr Janeki's sheep has been attacked by a dog,' Mrs Hope said with a worried frown.

Mandy's hand flew to her mouth. 'You don't think . . .'

Her mother's face was serious. 'Yes, I'm afraid so, Mandy. It could well have been Charley!'

Five

'But how do you know it could be Charley?' Mandy insisted. 'Surely she wouldn't do a thing like that?'

'Well, it was a black dog. It could have been her,' Mrs Hope said as the four-wheel drive headed for the village and Lilac Cottage. 'And you know, Mandy, if it *was* Charley, she could be shot.'

'I know.' Mandy's heart lurched with fear. 'That's why we've got to find her, Mum,' she said determinedly. 'As soon as possible.'

As they drew up outside the house, Mandy could see her grandfather mowing the lawn beneath the huge lilac tree that gave the cottage its name. Mandy loved the smell of new-cut grass. It reminded her of summery days and Gran's homemade lemonade on the lawn.

Mandy, James and Jess climbed out of the car and went through the front gate.

'This grass seems to grow as fast as I cut it,' Grandad said stopping the mower's engine and giving Mandy a hug. 'Hiya James,' he added with a grin.

'Hello, Mr Hope,' James said cheerfully.

Grandad bent to stroke Jess. 'Hello, Jack Russell. She's getting fat, Mandy.'

'I know. Dad says I'm feeding her too much, but she always seems to be hungry.'

Grandad waved goodbye to Mrs Hope as she drew away from the kerb. 'Come on, you two. Let's go and find your gran. The smell of that chocolate cake's been driving me mad all morning.' He ushered them past his bicycle leaning up against the wall, past the fragrant herb garden and into the warm and cosy cottage kitchen. 'The camper's in for a service,' he explained, 'so I've been using my bike to go into Walton.

'They're here, Dorothy!' Grandad called. Mandy could hear the sound of music and someone giving some kind of instructions. 'She's doing her aerobics,' Grandad said with a wink. 'Dorothy!' He disappeared into the back room. Mandy heard the video recorder being switched off. A moment later Gran appeared in her green tracksuit, looking red in the face.

She gave Mandy a hug. 'Mandy! It's great to see you. And you, James. Now, how about a slice of cake?'

She went to the pantry and brought out a huge chocolate cake with orange icing on the top. Mandy saw James's eyes open wide in amazement. 'Fancy some milk as well?' asked Gran.

'Yes, please,' they chorused. Mandy tried her best to look cheerful but she saw her grandmother glance knowingly at her worried face.

'What's up, Mandy?' Gran cut four slices of cake and put them on pretty porcelain plates. 'Tell us what's wrong.'

Suddenly it all poured out: the visit to Bleakfell

Hall; how George Sims had let poor Charley out in the thunderstorm; how she had gone missing; how they had searched in vain.

'And Mr Janeki's sheep have been attacked,' Mandy added, close to tears. 'We're really scared it might be Charley, aren't we, James?'

James nodded, his mouth full of cake.

'. . . and now we're going to ask round the village and make some posters saying Charley's missing,' Mandy added. 'Can you think of anything else we can do, Gran?'

'I'd have taken you out in the camper to look for her if it was here,' Grandad said.

'Never mind, Grandad,' Mandy said with a sigh. 'It can't be helped.'

Mandy's grandmother looked thoughtful. 'You know they have a programme on local radio where you can phone in. Maybe you could do that, Mandy – put out a message about Charley?' She rose and went to the sideboard. 'I've got their number written down in my telephone book.'

Grandad rose and wiped his mouth. 'That was really yummy, Dorothy. Oh, well, better finish that lawn before it rains.'

Mandy took Gran's telephone book and went

into the back room where the phone was. She dialled quickly. She felt a bit nervous. She had never spoken to anyone at a radio station before.

'Radio Yorkshire.' They answered straight away.

'Umm . . .' Mandy said. 'Could you put me through to the afternoon show, please.'

There were several clicks, then a man's voice answered. 'Yes. Can I help you?'

Mandy quickly explained about Charley. '. . . so if anyone sees a black Labrador with a red collar would they please ring Welford 703627.' Mandy felt quite breathless after rushing to tell the story.

'Yes, we'll put that out about three o'clock,' the man said.

'Oh, thank you,' Mandy breathed.

'Good luck,' the man said. Mandy heard another click as he put the phone down.

She went back into the kitchen. 'They're putting out a call on the afternoon show,' she said. 'That should help, shouldn't it?' She ran to hug her grandmother. 'Thanks, Gran, you're brilliant. Come on, James, let's go and ask if anyone's seen Charley round the village!'

Mandy's grandparents stood at the gate to wave goodbye.

'Where shall we go first?' James said, racing to keep up.

'We'll try the post office,' Mandy said.

The village post office sold more than just stamps. In fact it sold just about everything. Newspapers, groceries, pegs, sweets, even paper-clips.

The small bell clanged as Mandy went in. James stayed outside with Jess as dogs weren't allowed in the shop.

The postmistress, Mrs McFarlane, was behind the counter.

'Hello, Mandy.'

'Mrs McFarlane,' Mandy said. 'Have you seen a black Labrador dog at all?'

'You mean Blackie, James Hunter's dog? Has he got lost?'

Mandy shook her head. 'No . . . like Blackie, but a female dog. She's with the film company up at Bleakfell Hall but she's gone missing.'

Mrs McFarlane shook her head. She was a kindly lady and she knew everyone's business. If anyone had seen Charley, Mrs McFarlane would know. 'No, I'm sorry, Mandy, I haven't.'

'If we do a poster about her, would you put it in the window?'

Mrs McFarlane smiled. 'Of course, Mandy. I'd be glad to.'

'Thanks, Mrs McFarlane.' Mandy felt pleased. It was great to live in a place like Welford where everyone was willing to help out.

Outside, James waited. 'Any luck?'

Mandy shook her head. 'No, but they'll put a poster up for us.'

'Let's try Mr Oliver in the butcher's shop,' James suggested.

But they had no luck there either. They asked Ernie Bell who lived in the cottages behind the Fox and Goose but he hadn't seen Charley. Neither had Eileen Davy from the Old School House. Nor grumpy Mr Simmons, clipping the hedge in the churchyard. In fact no one had seen her. By the time they had asked almost everyone they knew, their task seemed hopeless.

'Come on, James,' Mandy said, feeling miserable again. 'Let's get back to Animal Ark and do those posters.'

Back at the cottage, Mandy found some paper

to make the posters. They sat down at the kitchen table.

'If we just do one,' Mandy said, chewing the end of her pen thoughtfully, 'Jean will let us make some photocopies to put up round the village. Any ideas, James?'

'How about this?' James wrote on a piece of scrap paper.

LOST THE FILM STAR DOG
'CHARLEY'
A female black Labrador dog
gone missing from Bleakfell Hall
If you see her please call
WELFORD 703267

'That looks great,' Mandy said delightedly. 'Good old James!'

James went a bit red.

Just then, Mr Hope came into the kitchen. 'What are you up to, you two?' he asked.

'We're making a poster about Charley to put up

round the village,' Mandy explained.

Mr Hope peered over James's shoulder at the poster. 'That's a good idea. Mum told me about Charley – I do hope she turns up.'

'So do we,' they chorused.

'Do you have to do it right now?' Mr Hope asked.

'Well, the sooner the better. Why?' Mandy asked curiously.

'Well, I've got to go up to the animal sanctuary. I thought you might like to come.'

'Mrs Platt's poodle!' Mandy exclaimed. In the worry over Charley she had forgotten all about it.

Adam Hope held up his hand. 'I don't know if they've actually got a poodle, Mandy, but it would be a good chance to ask. Someone's handed in a fox that's been injured; that's why I'm going.'

'Want to come, James?' Mandy said to her friend.

James shook his head. 'I'd like to but I'd better get back. My aunt's coming this afternoon. I could do the poster if you like. Then we could photocopy it when you get back.'

'Oh, James, that would be great.'

James rolled up the paper. 'See you later then,' he said, going out.

'Want to come with us, Jess?' Mandy bent down to stroke Jess, curled up in her basket.

'Leave her,' Mr Hope said. 'She looks tired out.'

Mandy frowned. 'I hope she's OK. She's been looking a bit droopy lately.'

'Hmm.' Mr Hope stroked his beard thoughtfully. 'Remind me, I'll take a look at her when we get back.'

Twenty minutes later Mandy and her father were bumping and rattling their way up the unmade road that led to the animal rescue centre. Mandy stared gloomily out of the window. All she could think of was Charley, running loose somewhere on the moors and dales. In the distance, she could see the far-away lumps of the Pennine Hills. White clouds had built up over their tops like raggy puffs of cotton wool in a clear blue sky.

'What happened to the fox?' Mandy asked, dragging her thoughts away from Charley.

'Caught in one of those wire snares, I'm afraid,' Mr Hope said with a grim look on his face.

Mandy's heart went out to the poor wild creature. 'I hate snares,' she announced angrily. 'They should be banned! I don't know how people can set them.'

They drove through the gate. The big sign said 'Welford Animal Sanctuary' with a picture of a donkey painted in grey.

Betty Hilder, the woman who ran the sanctuary, came out of one of the sheds to greet them. She wore a long floral skirt with a man's tweed jacket over the top and heavy boots. Her face was brown and weathered. A couple of rather skinny cats wound themselves round her legs as she walked.

'Thanks for coming, Adam.' She shook his hand. 'The fox is in the barn. Come and see.'

The injured fox lay in a wire cage in an old stone barn next to a row of kennels. It snarled in fear as they approached.

'I think it's got a broken leg,' Betty said. 'It won't let me near it.'

Mandy bent to look into the cage. She felt angry and upset that the fox had been injured. Why couldn't people just leave wild creatures in peace?

'Here.' As she stood up, Mr Hope handed

Mandy a strong pair of gloves from his bag. 'Put these on. We'll take a look.'

Mandy held the young fox's head firmly. Its coat was red and glossy with a beautiful white bib. Mr Hope quickly examined its swollen front leg.

'He's been licking it by the looks of it, Dad.' Mandy felt a surge of pity. The fox looked at her with fear in its black eyes.

'Yes. I'm afraid it needs more than just a lick to make it better,' Mr Hope said with a frown on his usually good-humoured face.

'It's OK,' Mandy said gently to the struggling

fox. 'We're not going to hurt you.'

'It's broken all right,' Mr Hope said. 'I'll give him an injection to make him sleep while I strap it up. Could we have a bowl of hot water please, Betty?'

Mandy held on firmly as Mr Hope injected the scared creature with a mild anaesthetic. Gradually, she felt it go limp. Its eyes closed as it fell asleep.

Betty came back with a bowl of steaming water.

'This won't take long.' Mr Hope took a roll of fine white mesh bandage from his bag.

'We soak this in the hot water,' he explained. 'It goes all soft and we wrap it round the broken leg.'

'Then when it dries,' Mandy went on, 'it sets hard, like a plaster.'

'How long will it have to be on there do you think?' Betty asked, after they had finished.

'A few weeks,' Mr Hope said. 'Then he should be as good as new.'

'Thanks, Adam, Mandy.' Betty smiled at them both.

'Keep him warm, plenty to drink.' Mr Hope stroked the glossy red fur while Mandy settled the fox back into its cage.

'How much do I owe you?' Betty asked.

Mr Hope patted Betty's arm. 'Nothing. I had to come up this way anyway.' He winked at Mandy. Her dad never charged the sanctuary. *But don't tell your mum,* the wink seemed to say.

They all went outside.

'Betty,' Mandy said, 'I don't suppose you have a poodle to adopt? Mrs Platt's just had to have hers put to sleep and she can't afford to buy a new one.'

'I'm sorry, we haven't, Mandy. Not at the moment,' Betty said. 'But I'll let you know if we get one.'

'Thanks,' Mandy said. 'Oh, and by the way, if you see a black Labrador, or if anyone brings one in, the film company up at Bleakfell Hall has lost one.'

'Oh, dear,' Betty said. 'Of course. I'll let you know if I hear of anything,' she promised.

Mandy took a last glance back at the rows of kennels as they drove away. She felt sad and angry that there were so many homeless animals in the world.

A couple of miles from the village, the car phone rang.

'Yup,' Mandy heard her dad say. 'Where? I'll tell her. Thanks, Jean.

'Mr Redpath's called Jean to say he's seen a black dog in one of his fields. Apparently it ran off towards the river,' Mr Hope explained.

'Oh, Dad!' Mandy's heart leapt with hope. 'It could be Charley. Did Mr Redpath say if it was wearing a collar?'

'Yes,' Mr Hope glanced at his daughter. 'A red one.'

'Yippee!' Mandy cried, clapping her hands together. 'Oh, Dad, it really could be her.'

Mandy's heart drummed all the way home. Charley was definitely still alive and in the area. It could only be a matter of time before they found her!

Six

'Can I turn the radio on, Dad?' Mandy asked as they neared the village.

'Yes, of course, Mandy.'

'I phoned Radio Yorkshire. They're going to put out a call for Charley on the afternoon show,' she explained. Mandy switched the radio on just as the show was ending.

'Oh,' Mandy felt disappointed. 'I would have loved to hear what they said.'

The announcer was still talking.

'Shh,' Mr Hope turned up the volume. 'Listen!'

'And just a reminder about that missing dog,' the announcer said. 'Her name's Charley and she's wearing a red collar. If you see her, phone Welford 703627 – there's a very anxious girl waiting desperately for news.'

Mandy looked at her father. 'It sounded great, didn't it?' She felt a surge of hope.

'Yes.' Mr Hope patted Mandy's knee. 'Let's hope it does the trick.'

Back at Animal Ark James was waiting.

'I managed to escape from Mum and my aunt,' he admitted. 'I said this was really urgent.'

'Well, it is.' Mandy told James about Mr Redpath seeing a dog with a red collar.

'It could be Charley!' James said excitedly.

'I know,' Mandy said. 'That's why we've got to get these up quick – so if anyone sees her they'll know who she is.'

James had written the poster in green marker pen with a drawing of a black Labrador on one side.

'Oh, James, it's brilliant! Come on, let's ask Jean if we can use the photocopier.'

They went through into the surgery reception.

Jean Knox was looking through the blue appointment book. She glanced up and smiled as Mandy and James came through.

'Can we use the photocopier please, Jean?' Mandy asked.

Jean took off her glasses. They swung on a silver chain against her hand-knitted pink cardigan. 'What is it, dear?' Jean was a bit fussy about the office machines.

'A poster,' Mandy explained. 'About Charley, the missing film star dog.'

'Yes, help yourselves.'

They went into the back room. The photocopier whirred as Mandy made a dozen copies.

'Where to first?' James asked as they hurried outside.

'I'm going to ask the vicar if we can put one on the parish notice-board,' Mandy said. 'It will be a great place. Everyone who comes to the village has to pass it.'

They made their way across the village green and down the short-cut beside the Fox and Goose. Old Walter Pickard was in the front garden of his little stone cottage, dead-heading his roses. His fat tom-cat was asleep on the front step in a pool of late afternoon sunshine. Walter was an old friend of Grandad's. Both of them had been church bell-ringers for years.

'Now then, you youngsters,' Walter called. 'Where are you off to?'

'Hello, Mr Pickard. We're just going to ask the vicar if he'll put one of these up.' Mandy showed Walter the poster.

'What's that all about then?'

Mandy quickly explained about Charley.

'Is she a star then? I haven't seen her.'

'Well,' Mandy said. 'She's a star to us because she's such a beautiful dog.'

'We thought it would make people take notice,' James added.

'Aye, it will that. Well, good luck, young miss. I'll keep an eye out for her.'

'Thanks, Mr Pickard.'

Outside the church, Mr Hadcroft, Welford's vicar, was just getting off his bicycle.

Mandy and James ran across.

'Well, hello, you two.' The vicar took off his crash-helmet. 'You look in a hurry.'

'Yes, we are a bit.' Mandy had suddenly realised

it was near closing time. In fifteen minutes or so the shops would be shut and the posters would have to wait until tomorrow. Her heart lurched to think Charley had been missing almost a whole day.

'Could you please put this poster up on the board,' Mandy begged. 'We'd be ever so grateful.'

Mr Hadcroft looked at the poster. 'Sure,' he said. He used several rusty drawing pins to pin up the poster. He stood back. 'That looks fine. Hope you have some luck with the dog.'

'Thanks!' Mandy and James chorused. They sprinted across the green to the post office.

Mrs McFarlane was counting the money in the till.

'Here's the poster about Charley,' Mandy said breathlessly.

'Leave it on the counter, dear,' Mrs McFarlane said, putting a pile of ten-pence pieces into a blue bag. 'I'll put it up when I've finished doing the money.'

Mandy and James dashed back to the grocer's, then to the butcher. Soon, every shop in the village had the poster in its window. They even stuck one on the huge oak tree by the village pond.

'Just in time,' James panted as the very last doorbell clanged behind them. 'Now we'll just have to wait to see what happens.'

'I'll phone Bleakfell Hall tonight and tell them what we've done,' said Mandy. 'I've just got time to do my chores before tea.'

At Animal Ark, evening surgery was just beginning. Mandy popped her head round the door.

'We're back,' she said to her mum. Mrs Hope was sitting at the bench counting sterile-packed hypodermic needles. She looked up. 'Where from?'

'We've been putting posters about Charley all round the village.'

'Well done, Mandy.' Mrs Hope replaced the box on the shelf. 'Hope it does the trick.'

As they passed the treatment room Mandy saw Jess up on the table. Mr Hope was just finishing examining her.

'Is she OK, Dad?' Mandy went in to stroke the terrier.

Mr Hope glanced at Mandy's anxious face. 'She's fine, Mandy.' He smiled. 'She's absolutely fine.'

'That's good.' Mandy heaved a sigh of relief. A

missing Labrador and a sick terrier would just be too much to cope with!

Later, after James had gone home for supper, Mandy rang Bleakfell Hall. She was so anxious for news of Charley she had hardly been able to eat a thing.

Luckily, Ben Burton, Mr Curtis's assistant, answered.

'Oh, hello, Mandy. I don't suppose you've heard anything about the dog, have you?'

'No,' Mandy said. 'That's why I'm ringing. I hoped *you* had.'

'No – nothing. And Animal Stars haven't got another black Labrador available. I really don't know what we're going to do!'

Mandy's heart sank. In spite of the posters, the call to the local radio, she had still been holding on to a desperate hope that Charley might find her way back to Bleakfell Hall on her own.

'One of the local farmers saw a black Labrador,' she told Ben. 'I hoped it was Charley but we haven't heard anything since.' She glanced at the clock over the inglenook fireplace. It was eight-thirty, almost twenty-four hours since Charley ran off!

'I know you're upset about her,' Ben was saying, 'but we've got to get on with filming. I don't suppose you know of another dog we could use, Mandy?'

'Well,' Mandy said, an idea occurring to her. 'My friend James has got a black Labrador.'

'Great! Is he obedient?'

'Well . . .' Mandy hesitated. Should she tell a little white lie? James would be so proud if Blackie was in a film. 'Yes, he's not *too* bad.' It wasn't a fib at all, really. Blackie wasn't too bad at doing as he was told. Just not too good, either.

'Could you bring him up? We could give it a try,' Ben said, sounding pleased.

'I should think that'll be OK. I'll ask.'

'Mandy, you're wonderful. Mr Curtis will be so happy.' Ben sounded delighted. 'Can you come tomorrow?'

'I expect so,' Mandy said. 'I'll ring James now if you like. I'm sure my dad will bring us.'

'Fine,' said Ben. 'See you in the morning.'

James was full of excitement when she phoned to tell him what Ben Burton had said.

'I'll get up early and give Blackie a bath,' James said. 'He rolled in some manure this morning so he's not allowed indoors at the moment.'

'Trust him,' Mandy said. She put the phone down with a sigh. It was all very well Blackie being Charley's stand-in. But what they really needed was Charley herself!

Very early next morning James and a super-clean Blackie were on the doorstep.

'Wow! You're early,' Mandy said as she answered James's knock on the door.

'It's not every day Blackie gets his big chance,' James said proudly.

Mr Hope came through from the surgery. 'I'm taking you up to Bleakfell Hall,' he said. 'Mum's busy with surgery this morning. I've just got to load the Land-rover up. We've got to call in at Sunrise Farm on the way – a cow's down with milk-fever.'

When they arrived at Sunrise Farm, Mr Jones, the farmer, came out from the angular grey-stone farmhouse to greet them. He had an empty tobacco-pipe in his mouth. Mandy had never seen him without it. It hissed and bubbled like a kettle as he sucked.

'Make sure Blackie stays in the car,' Mr Hope

warned. 'We don't want the cow getting upset, especially as she has a new calf.'

'Went down early this morning,' Mr Jones explained. *Suck, suck, hiss, bubble.* 'We tried to get her up but it's no good.'

In the barn, a cream and brown Jersey cow was lying in the straw. Her legs were folded up underneath her stomach. They had propped her up with a couple of straw bales to stop her rolling over. By her side stood a soft-eyed calf barely more than a few hours old. It mooed softly and wobbled away on unsteady legs. There was a sweet smell of fresh milk and hay.

Mr Hope knelt down beside the mother cow. He ran his hands over her flanks.

'OK, old girl,' he said. 'We'll soon have you on your feet.'

Mandy knew what was needed. 'Shall I get the bottle of calcium from your bag, Dad?'

'Yes, please, Mandy. And a needle and a tube.'

'Milk-fever's caused by a sudden loss of calcium,' Mr Hope explained to a wide-eyed James. 'It happens soon after a new calf is born. I'll inject some calcium into the cow and she'll soon be as good as new.'

Mr Hope took the needle from Mandy and attached it to a long, thin rubber tube. Then he fixed the other end to a bottle. He quickly stuck the needle into one of the cow's veins.

'Hold it up please, Mandy.'

As the calcium flowed into the cow's blood, she began to stir. After a while Mr Hope pulled out the needle. He wiped his hands on his overalls. 'OK, stand back, she's going to get up.'

Mandy held her breath. The cow struggled to her feet. Mandy's heart pounded. Would the cow fall again? She had helped her father do this many times and knew it was always an anxious moment.

The mother cow was swaying about in the sun-yellow straw like a great ship on the sea. Then she seemed to get her balance. She moved forward as her calf came trotting. She mooed softly. A new sucking noise came as the calf greedily drank its mother's milk.

Mandy breathed a sigh of relief. It was times like this, knowing she could really help to save an animal's life, that made her more keen than ever to be a vet herself.

'Thanks, Adam.' Mr Jones looked relieved.

Suck, suck, bubble, bubble went his empty pipe.
'I can't afford to lose such a good milker. Well
done, Mandy. I can see you're going to make a
great vet yourself one day.' *Bubble . . . bubble . . .*

Mandy blushed with pride.

'We're on our way to Bleakfell Hall,' Mandy
heard her father say.

'Any sign of their missing dog? I heard about it
when I went into the post office yesterday,' Mr
Jones said.

'Not yet. We're keeping our fingers crossed. In
the meantime James's dog is going to act as a
stand-in.'

The farmer grinned then sucked even harder
on his empty pipe. 'Good luck!'

But things didn't quite go as Mandy expected.

As they drew up outside Bleakfell Hall, the
front door suddenly flew open. Out surged a
stream of people led by a woman in a white silk
frock.

'That's Antonia Kent,' Mandy whispered to her
father. 'What's happened now?'

Antonia Kent strode towards them in a swathe
of silk. After her ran Hammond Curtis, clipboard
held aloft. Today, a red bandana replaced his

usual baseball cap. After *him* ran Ben Burton, holding out what looked like a mug of tea. Next came one of the production assistants. Then Mandy gasped with surprise as a man in an old-fashioned frock coat and top hat came running out. His white shirt was covered in blood. Sticking out from his chest was a ruby handled dagger although he was striding along like a healthy athlete.

Last but not least, there was a flurry of red and green. Mr Baggins the parrot!

'Mr Baggins.' Mandy climbed hastily from the Land-rover. She ran towards the parrot. 'Mr Baggins!'

With a screech the bright bird flew over Antonia's head. She crouched down on the driveway, hands waving like a windmill.

'Beastly thing! Take it away, someone!'

'*Good morning!*' Mr Baggins screeched. '*Where's Charley?*' With that he promptly landed on Mandy's head.

'There you are,' Miss Kent said dramatically. Her nose was up in the air, her wig falling over one eye. 'If this girl's so good with animals, *she* can star in this dreadful film. I'm leaving!'

Seven

'What on earth's going on?' Mr Hope's mouth fell open when he saw the procession of people pour out of Bleakfell Hall.

'Come down, Mr Baggins,' Mandy commanded. The naughty parrot stepped on to her fingers. Then he hopped off on to her shoulder.

'*Where's the cup tea. I wanna be a yeah, yeah,*' Mr Baggins murmured in her ear.

The director, Hammond Curtis, was trying to soothe Antonia Kent with a mug of tea. They were sitting on the stone steps, talking earnestly.

'I'm sure the parrot will behave itself now Mandy's here,' Mr Curtis was saying. Mandy saw him wink at her over the actress's shoulder.

'He tried to peck my beauty spot.' Antonia sniffed, wiping her eyes.

'He thought it was a sunflower seed – now please calm down, Antonia.' Mr Curtis patted Antonia Kent's shaking shoulder.

Mandy tried not to laugh out loud. 'We've brought Blackie,' she managed to splutter.

Mr Hope had gone round to the stables to look at one of the horses that had gone lame. Blackie was sitting, good as gold, at James's feet.

Suddenly Mr Curtis stood up. He clapped his hands. 'OK, everyone, back inside. I've managed to persuade Miss Kent to carry on and Charley's understudy has arrived by the look of it. Let's get on with the job, shall we?'

They all filed back indoors. Mr Curtis waited for Mandy and James.

'This is Blackie, is it?' He gave the dog a pat. 'Thanks for bringing him, young man.'

'That's OK,' James mumbled shyly.

'I hope he's going to be obedient.'

'Oh, no – yes, I mean.' James went red.

'I expect he will,' Mandy said hastily. 'For the first time ever,' she whispered under her breath.

'I've been training him,' James said, looking up at Mr Curtis.

'Good man.' Mr Curtis slapped James on the shoulder.

Suddenly, with a squawk Mr Baggins took off. Up into the chandelier. A screech filled the air.

Mandy heard a groan from the crew.

'OK, OK,' Mr Curtis shouted. 'Leave him there for the time being.'

Someone stepped forward with a black and white clapperboard.

'Take your places!' Mr Curtis ordered.

The man with the dagger in his chest lay backwards on the hall table. Someone ran over with a bottle. He splashed gooey red liquid on the floor.

'Not too much,' Mr Curtis called. 'It's not a horror film.'

He beckoned to James. 'Can you get your dog to lie by the fireplace, young man?'

'I'll try,' James said.

Mandy held her breath. She suddenly

remembered all the trouble Blackie had caused at this year's Welford Show, snatching Mrs Ponsonby's hat and running riot in the show ring. 'Oh, Blackie,' she whispered. 'Please be good!'

James led Blackie towards the big stone fireplace. He unclipped his lead. 'Stay!' he commanded. James fished about in the pocket of his track suit trousers. He held up a biscuit. 'Stay!' he commanded again.

Blackie lay down, head on paws. His eyes roamed the room. Mandy's heart was in her mouth.

Blackie stared up at Mr Baggins. Mr Baggins

stared down at Blackie. James backed away from the dog, hand raised. Blackie lay still. *It's going to be all right*, Mandy thought. *It's really going to be all right!*

Ben took Mandy aside. 'This is the scene just after the murder,' he whispered. 'Blackie . . . er, Black Rose and Mr Baggins are the only witnesses.'

'Oh,' Mandy whispered. Miss Kent looked angry enough to stab someone for real.

'Then she removes the dagger and hides it in the cupboard. But Black Rose sniffs it out.'

'Oh, dear!' Mandy's eyes were wide. 'I'm not sure . . .'

'What?' Ben asked.

'Nothing,' Mandy said. She thought perhaps it was the wrong time to tell Ben that the only thing Blackie was good at sniffing out was his dinner!

'We got to this bit before you arrived,' Ben went on. 'But Mr Baggins took a sudden fancy to that beauty spot on Antonia Kent's cheek.'

Mandy giggled. She wouldn't have missed this for anything!

'Silence!' Mr Curtis yelled.

Antonia Kent took her position by the corpse. The clapperboard clapped.

They were ready.

Antonia Kent pretended to look round warily. Then, still glancing over her shoulder, she began to remove the dagger from the man's chest.

A sudden commotion from the first floor landing made her freeze in her tracks. The three cats came hurtling down the staircase. In front, a little grey mouse fled in terror. They sped across the hall and through the door.

Mr Baggins squawked in alarm. '*She loves tea!*' he screeched. '*Where's Charley?*'

Antonia Kent screamed. 'A mouse . . . a mouse!' Up went her long skirts. She jumped on to the table in one great leap.

It was all too much for Blackie. First the parrot; then the cats; now a screaming, jumping woman. He barked, leapt to his feet, hared after the cats. His claws scratched the wooden floor as he slipped and scrambled his way to the kitchen.

'Cut!' Mr Curtis yelled.

Mandy snorted with laughter. Mr Curtis put his head into his hands. The man with the dagger in his chest stood up and lit a cigarette. In one corner, a young woman dressed as a Victorian parlour-maid took a can of Coke from behind a potted plant and raised it to her lips.

Mandy wiped her eyes. James disappeared towards the kitchen after Blackie. Ben Burton was doubled up, laughing his head off. Antonia Kent swept up the stairs in a flurry of long skirts and hurt pride. The scene was ruined.

Mandy ran after James.

In the kitchen, George Sims had hold of Blackie's collar. The Labrador was sitting at his feet, looking sorry for himself. James was telling him off.

'Blackie!' He shook his finger at the dog. Mr Sims let go of his collar and Blackie lay down beside him.

George Sims scratched his head. 'I thought it was Charley coming through that door,' he said.

'I'm afraid not.' Mandy gave Blackie a hug. He might not be a good actor, but he was a great one for cheering people up. She looked up at Mr Sims. 'No sign of Charley, then?'

Mr Sims shook his head. 'If she don't turn up soon. I'm likely to lose my job,' he said, looking sorry for himself.

'We put a call out on the local radio,' Mandy said. 'And put posters up in the village.'

'Well, thanks for your help,' Mr Sims said gruffly. 'I know I was daft to let her out. I'm just not used to animals.'

'When are they sending your replacement?' Mandy began to feel sorry for George Sims. He really wasn't so bad. And she could see by the look on his face that he would never have frightened Charley on purpose.

Mr Sims shrugged. 'Tomorrow, I hope. There's something wrong with one of the horses now. I thought parrots were enough trouble.' He shook his head. 'I just can't cope with it. If I didn't have a wife and four kids, I'd quit the job.'

Mandy suddenly had an idea. 'Mr Sims,' she said. 'If you like, James and I will help out with the animals. Just until the new person comes that is.'

George Sims seemed to cheer up a bit. A grin spread across his face. 'Now, that's not a bad idea. Them horses need mucking out but—' His face fell. '—I couldn't pay you anything.'

Mandy waved her hand. 'No, we wouldn't want paying, would we, James?'

'Er . . . no,' James said, although Mandy didn't think he looked very certain.

George Sims beamed. 'All right, you're on.' He looked over his shoulder. 'I expect I could run to getting you a few ice creams.'

Mandy grinned. 'Thanks, Mr Sims.'

Just then, Hammond Curtis came into the kitchen. Mr Baggins sat on his shoulder. Mandy only just managed to suppress a giggle. Mr Curtis only needed a wooden leg and an eye patch and he'd look like Long John Silver!

'I think everyone's calmed down now,' he said. 'Thanks for bringing your dog, James. I'm sorry, I don't think he'll be suitable after all.'

James's face fell. 'I am *trying* to train him, honestly.'

Mandy felt sorry for James – and for Blackie. He'd lost his big chance to be a star.

'Of course, what we really need,' Mr Curtis said, glaring at George Sims, 'is Charley! If she's not found, I don't know *what* we're going to do!'

Mr Sims hung his head.

Mr Curtis put Mr Baggins back on his perch. 'You'd better round up the cats, George. Goodness knows where they've all got to.'

'And we'll go and find my dad, and ask him if we can stay and help with the animals,' Mandy said.

Mr Hope was just washing his hands under the yard tap.

'Dad,' Mandy said excitedly. 'We're going to stay and help George. Is that OK?'

'Yes, of course it is. I'll pick you up later if you like. How did Blackie's debut go?'

James blushed. 'He failed his audition.'

'Oh, dear.' Mr Hope's eyes twinkled. 'I must say I'm not surprised. That dog's too intelligent to let anyone boss him around.'

James brightened. 'That's right,' he said proudly. 'Thank you, Mr Hope.'

A couple of hours later everything was spick and span. Mandy and James had mucked out and put clean bedding in the stables. They had fed the horses, and the cats, which they'd found in the cellar standing guard over a mouse-hole in the skirting-board. James had swept the yard while Mandy sat by the fire in the kitchen grooming the cats. She giggled, thinking about Blackie and Mr Baggins and poor Antonia Kent. How could anyone be scared of a tiny little mouse?

When Mr Hope arrived to collect them, Mandy and James were eating ice creams in the kitchen. Mr Baggins was asleep, his head tucked under his wing.

'Don't know what I'd have done without them.' George Sims said as Mr Hope came through the door. 'They can work for Animal Stars any time!'

'Can we come back tomorrow, Dad?' Mandy asked.

'Yes, fine. I've got to go to Walton Market in the afternoon. I'll drop you off on the way,' Mr Hope said.

'Thanks, Dad.' Mandy's eyes shone. 'You're the best.'

'*Where's the tea?*' Mr Baggins mumbled sleepily.

Mr Hope dropped James and Blackie off at their gate on the way back to Animal Ark.

'See you tomorrow, James,' Mandy called, waving goodbye.

When they arrived home, Mr Hope went off to make out his report. Mandy greeted Jess in the kitchen. The terrier was in her basket. She looked up and wagged her tail as Mandy came in but didn't climb out. Mandy frowned. Jess really was out of sorts lately. She hoped her dad had been right when he said she was OK.

'A long walk might be what you need, Jess,' Mandy said, stroking her wiry coat. 'You're not getting enough exercise, that's the trouble. I'll take you in the morning if you're good.'

She gave the dog a hug then went through into the surgery. Simon was sterilising the surgical instruments.

'Oh, Mandy,' he said as she came in. 'There was a telephone call for you.'

'Who from?' Mandy asked curiously.

'I don't know – ask Jean.' Simon opened the steriliser to a cloud of steam.

Mandy went through to reception. Jean was sitting at her typewriter, a frown on her face. She was trying to work out Mr Hope's spidery handwriting on a sheet of paper beside her machine.

'Jean, Simon says there was a call for me,' Mandy said eagerly.

'Oh, yes.' Jean flicked through her shorthand pad. '. . . Here it is. Betty from the animal sanctuary. She asked you to call her.'

Mandy's heart leapt. It might be news about Charley!

'Use my phone if you like,' Jean went on. 'The sanctuary's number is on the notice-board above your head.'

Mandy was so excited she could hardly dial the number.

'Animal sanctuary, Betty speaking.'

'Betty,' Mandy said breathlessly. 'There's a message for me to ring you.'

Betty recognised her voice. 'Hi, Mandy,' she said cheerfully. 'I thought you'd like to know the RSPCA have brought in a stray poodle. She might do for your friend, Mrs Platt.'

'That's great, Betty,' Mandy said, brushing aside her disappointment at there being no news of Charley. 'Could we come up and see her?'

'Yes, sure,' Betty replied. 'Whenever you like.'

'I'll ask if Mum or Dad can bring me. We'll come as soon as we can.'

'OK, Mandy. I'll be here,' said Betty.

Mandy put the phone down. She looked at her watch. If her mum wasn't busy she just might take her up to the sanctuary before surgery.

Mandy hurried through into the kitchen. Mrs Hope was folding her white vet's coat.

'Mum!' Mandy burst out. 'Is there time for us

to go up to the animal sanctuary before surgery?'

Mrs Hope glanced up at the clock. 'Yes, I should think so. Why?'

'Betty's just phoned. She's got a poodle for Mrs Platt. Can we go and see her?'

Mrs Hope put her vet's coat on the shelf. 'That's great news. I'll just get my keys.'

She came back a minute later. 'Come on then, sweetheart. Let's go and take a look at this poodle.'

Eight

Mandy fidgeted all the way to the animal sanctuary. Her eyes darted from side to side, as they drove along, still looking for signs of Charley. To find Charley and a poodle for Mrs Platt all in one day would be like a dream come true.

At the animal sanctuary, Betty ushered them into the house. The poodle, thin and weak, lay in a basket in front of Betty's fire.

'Oh . . .' Mandy knelt down beside the basket. She gently touched the poodle's matted grey coat.

Her heart turned over with pity.

'She had been left tied to a tree over at Monkton Spinney,' Mandy heard Betty saying to Mrs Hope. 'Luckily someone spotted her and took her to the RSPCA. She probably wouldn't have survived another night.'

'How could anyone do such a thing!' Mandy said, her voice barely a whisper.

She heard her mother sigh. 'Don't ask me, Mandy. I don't know either.'

Mandy looked up at Betty and her mother. They were standing watching her stroke the poodle. Mrs Hope's face was full of sadness.

'Do you think she'll be OK, Mum?' Mandy asked anxiously. She had seen abandoned animals before but never one who looked quite so thin and ill.

Her mother crouched down beside her. She quickly ran her hands over the little dog then looked into her eyes and ears.

'It's hard to say,' said Mrs Hope. 'She's suffering from exposure.' She lifted the dog's muzzle to look at her teeth. 'A few good meals and a day or so in the warm and we'll take another look at her, OK?'

'Oh, *thanks*, Mum.' Mandy gave her mother a hug. 'She's got to be OK, she's just got to be!'

Mandy stroked the poodle gently. It raised its head weakly and licked her hand.

'There you are!' Mandy stood up. 'I know she's a little fighter!'

'She's had some warm milk and cereal,' said Betty. 'And what she really needs too is lots of love.'

'Mrs Platt will give her that, won't she, Mum?' Mandy said, trying to imagine Mrs Platt's delighted face when they turned up with a new dog for her.

'She certainly will,' Mrs Hope said. 'But, Mandy, I think we'd better make sure the dog is going to get really well before we tell Mrs Platt.'

'Whatever you say, Mum. I'll come up and see her again. I'll bring my pocket money next time. It will help pay for her food.'

'That is kind, Mandy,' Betty gave her a hug.

They left the poodle lying in her warm basket and went outside.

'I'm sorry, Mandy,' Mrs Hope said. 'We must get back. It's time for surgery.'

They waved goodbye to Betty and set off towards

Welford. Along the lane, Mrs Hope slowed down while two girl riders trotted past.

'Hello, Mrs Hope,' one of the girls called. It was Susan Collins, a new girl in the area. She had had a difficult time settling in at first, but she now looked completely at home.

Mrs Hope wound down her window. 'Hello, Susan. How's Prince these days?'

'Fine thank you,' Susan replied.

Mandy waved as the girls trotted smartly on.

For the rest of the journey home, Mandy was very thoughtful.

'You're quiet, Mandy,' Mrs Hope remarked.

'I was just thinking about Charley and that little poodle,' she said gloomily. 'Sometimes I think I'll never make a good vet – I get too upset.'

Mrs Hope patted her daughter's knee. 'Yes, you will, Mandy. I know you will. You'd make a very *bad* vet if you didn't care about your patients.'

Mandy sniffed, feeling a bit better. 'Yes, I suppose you're right.' She thought for a minute. She smiled at her mother. Mum always had the knack of saying the right thing. 'You know, Mum,' Mandy said, 'I think I'll call the poodle Antonia.'

Mrs Hope smiled. 'That's a very grand name. Why Antonia?'

'After that actress at Bleakfell Hall. She reminds me of a poodle with her hair tied up on the top of her head like that.'

'That's a bit cheeky, Mandy,' Mrs Hope said.

'No it's not,' Mandy replied indignantly. 'Poodles are beautiful. I think it's a compliment!'

The following morning, Mandy was putting out food for her rabbits when James arrived with Blackie. They were off on that walk Mandy had promised Jess.

The terrier barked with joy at seeing Blackie. The two dogs greeted each other with sniffs and wagging tails then ran off, chasing madly round and round the lawn.

'Mind the plants!' Mandy called. 'Control your dog, James!' she said with a grin.

'Some hope,' James muttered. He whistled to Blackie but the Labrador ignored him as usual.

'Where shall we go for our walk?' Mandy asked.

James shrugged. 'Up to you.'

They went into the kitchen to fetch Jess's lead. Mr Hope was reading his veterinary magazine at the table.

'Where are you two off to?' he asked as they came through the door.

'We're taking Jess on a long walk to try to get rid of that fat tummy.' Mandy bent to hug the Jack Russell.

Mr Hope shut his magazine and rose from the table. 'Well, I must go. I've got several calls to make. Mind how you go, you two. Take good care of Jess.'

Mandy frowned as her father went out. That was a funny thing to say. He *knew* she always took great care of the little Jack Russell. Mandy shrugged. Oh, well, her dad did say funny things sometimes. She took Jess's lead from its hook.

'Come on, you two.' Blackie and Jess were wagging their tails at each other and panting after their race round the garden. 'Let's go.'

They walked along the lane to the post office.

'I'm just going to get some penny chews.' James produced a ten-pence piece from his pocket.

They tied the dogs up outside.

'Hello, you two,' Mr McFarlane said from behind the counter. 'Any news of that dog from Bleakfell Hall yet, Mandy?'

Mandy shook her head sadly. 'Not yet, but we're keeping our fingers crossed.'

Outside, James gave Mandy five penny chews and they set off across the village green. Jess and Blackie strained at their leads.

'Let's go past the War Memorial,' Mandy said, pulling Jess back. 'Down by the pub and along the river. We can let them off along there.'

'Great,' James said.

They stopped briefly on the bridge to throw sticks into the river, then they climbed over the stile and wandered down to the river's edge. Mandy loved the sound of the water as it sang and bubbled over the stones. The level was high, swollen from last week's rain. Mandy unclipped Jess's lead.

'Off you go – and stay where we can see you!' she said sternly.

Jess bounded off, Blackie at her heels. They sniffed along the bank, darting to and fro as they caught the scent of a rabbit.

Suddenly, Mandy saw Jess scramble down to the river's edge. Blackie followed, his tail waving like a flag.

Then, all at once, Mandy saw Jess stand stock-still. Her head was cocked to one side.

'What's Jess heard?' James asked.

Mandy frowned. 'I don't know. Let's go and see.'

They scrambled down the bank. Mandy saw the alert little terrier standing like a statue at the water's edge.

Suddenly, Jess shot forward like a rocket.

'Hey!' Mandy yelled. She felt frightened that Jess might run off, and one missing dog was quite enough! 'Jess! Jess!' she shouted. 'Come back!'

But the terrier ignored her. She splashed across the stepping-stones and scrambled madly up the high bank on the other side of the river.

'Come on, James,' Mandy said urgently. 'We'd better go after her.'

James whistled to Blackie. The Labrador bounded towards him. For once it seemed Blackie was going to be obedient. Then he saw Jess's white tail disappearing over the top of the bank.

He gave a couple of loud barks and set off after her.

'Blackie!' James cried. He turned, but Mandy was already clambering down the bank, across the stepping-stones and up the hill on the other side.

'Wait for me!' he called, running after her.

'Come on,' she called. Her heart was pounding as she ran. 'Jess! Jess!'

By now both dogs had disappeared. Gone!

Through the spinney there was no sign of either of them. A rock-strewn hill lay ahead.

Side by side, Mandy and James scrambled up the hill after the dogs. At the top, they stood on a huge outcrop of rock. Below, the houses in the village looked small, like a doll's town.

Mandy listened. All she could hear was the faraway sound of a train. Surely Jess wouldn't be chasing that? She whirled round, looking in all directions. There was no sign of either dog. Where on earth had they gone?

Then, from behind a distant boulder, Mandy suddenly heard Jess's short, sharp bark.

She jumped down. 'Come on, James, this way!'

They ran towards the sound of Jess's frantic

barks. They dashed across the turf, scrambling over rocks.

'They're over there.' James pointed. 'Look – Blackie's tail is sticking out from behind that rock!'

'Oh, thank goodness.' Mandy heaved a sigh of relief. Now they could hear Jess and see Blackie's waving tail, she was beginning to feel a bit angry with the naughty dogs. Jess would get a good telling-off when they finally caught up with her.

Behind the rock, Jess still barked. A high, excited kind of bark that Mandy had never heard before.

They ran round the other side, then stopped dead in their tracks.

'Oh!' Mandy stood, hand over her mouth in disbelief.

For there, lying on her side beside a big grey boulder, was Charley! Her hind leg was caught in a snare.

Mandy's heart missed a beat. She could hardly believe what she was seeing.

Charley's sad eyes looked up at her as if to say 'Am I glad to see you!'

Mandy fell to her knees. Her throat felt choked

with joy and relief. 'Charley . . . Charley . . .' She
blinked back tears.

The dog's back leg was bleeding where the
tight wire held it fast. Mandy touched her gently.
Charley wagged her tail and licked Mandy's hand.
She tried to get up but fell back as the sharp wire
dug deeper into her leg. Mandy gasped as she saw
the blood ooze.

'Oh, poor Charley!' She looked up at James,
her heart filled with anger and pity.

'What are we going to do?' James gulped,
kneeling quickly beside Mandy. Jess and Blackie
were lying down, panting from their run.

Mandy wrenched off her jacket and lay it over the dog to keep her warm.

Mandy knew they had to get help. They would never manage to carry Charley back themselves. 'I'm going to find Mum or Dad,' she said quickly, her heart thumping in her chest. 'Stay with her, James. Keep Jess and Blackie with you.' She thrust the dog leads at him.

Mandy sped away. The wind blew back her short hair. She flew down the hill as fast as her legs would carry her. She splashed over the stepping-stones, heedless of wet feet and the chilly wind blowing through her sweatshirt. Mandy's breath came out in gasps. Past the village hall, the shops . . . the sleepy morning high street. Her heart seemed to be drumming, *hurry . . . hurry.*

She reached Animal Ark, thrust open the gate and dashed down the front path. She burst into the reception area. The door hit the wall with a clang.

'Where's Dad . . . Mum . . . Simon . . . anyone?' she panted to a startled Jean Knox.

Jean dropped her spectacles in surprise. 'Mandy, what on earth's happened? You look—'

'Please . . . where's . . .' She was completely out of breath.

'Your dad's just got back. He's in his surgery, but—'

Mandy didn't wait to hear any more. She rushed through to the back room.

Mr Hope was filling his bag with veterinary supplies.

'Dad! Dad! You've got to come. Quick!' Mandy gasped. 'We've found Charley!'

Mr Hope's eyes widened in surprise. 'Charley? Where is she?' As he was speaking, he closed his bag quickly and grabbed his car keys from the shelf.

Mandy tugged his arm. 'Quickly . . . oh, please. She's up on the hill. I'll show you as we go.'

They both ran through reception and out of the front door.

'If there's any calls I'll be back soon,' Mr Hope shouted to Jean Knox as they raced down the path.

They both leapt into the Land-rover.

'We went over the stile by the stone bridge,' Mandy explained. 'Jess ran off – she must have heard Charley whining.' Mandy felt so upset she began to sob. 'Oh, Dad, her leg's caught in a snare – it's horrible. Poor Charley.'

Mr Hope was bent over the wheel. The Land-rover roared up the high street and out towards the bridge. Mandy twisted her hands together anxiously. 'Dad, hurry . . . please hurry!'

Nine

Mr Hope screeched to a halt on the bridge. They both leapt out, clambered quickly over the stile and ran along the riverbank.

'This way,' Mandy panted as she plunged down the bank and splashed across the stepping-stones. She began the steep climb up the other side.

'Hang on!' her father called. Mandy was way ahead.

Mandy stopped and turned impatiently. 'Come *on*, Dad, for goodness' sake!' She held out her hand. Her father took it and together they ran through the spinney, out the other side and on up the steep bank towards the place where Charley lay injured.

'How much farther?' Mr Hope panted.

'Just there!' Mandy pointed to the pile of boulders past the steep outcrop of rock. 'Charley's over there!'

At the sound of her voice, Jess and Blackie came bounding up. Jess barked madly, jumping up at Mandy as she ran.

Mandy and Mr Hope arrived at last, breathless and flushed with running all the way from the road.

James leapt to his feet, looking mighty relieved. 'I thought you were never coming!'

'We've been as quick as we could,' Mandy panted.

Mr Hope knelt beside the injured Labrador. Charley wagged her tail feebly and whined. Mandy knelt beside them, clasping her hands together anxiously.

'Now then, old girl,' Mr Hope said gently. 'Let's have a look at you.' He eyed the snare with disgust. 'Who on earth . . . ?'

James shrugged. 'Don't ask me,' he said. 'Some idiot, I expect.'

Mr Hope took pliers from his bag. A couple of quick snips . . . the wire was gone.

'She's been trying to bite it off,' Mr Hope said almost to himself as he examined the wound.

'How long do you think she's been here, Dad?' Mandy felt better now her father was here. If anyone could make Charley OK, he could.

Mr Hope shook his head. 'Not that long – thank goodness. She's a bit thin. Been out on the moors, I should think. It's my guess she was heading back to the village. If she'd been here all the time I'm afraid she'd be dead by now.'

He quickly covered the wound with a rough bandage. 'That'll keep it clean while we carry her back to the car,' he said. 'I'll dress it properly when we get her to the Ark.'

Mr Hope fastened his bag and handed it to Mandy. 'Here, you carry this. He put his arms under the injured dog and lifted her up. She lay quietly in his arms. Her head lolled to one side. Big brown eyes looked at Mandy. Her tail wagged feebly. 'You lead, James,' said Mr Hope.

They set off down the hill in single file. James in front, Mandy behind, her heart pounding anxiously.

A couple of times, Mr Hope slipped on the damp turf. Mandy gasped and dashed forward to steady him, afraid he would stumble and fall with Charley in his arms. After that, she stuck beside her father like glue, guiding him over the uneven ground.

In front, Blackie and Jess trotted beside James as good as gold. Mandy was sure that somehow they realised the seriousness of the situation.

Crossing the river was worse. The stones were slippery at the best of times without having to carry a heavy dog in your arms. Mr Hope couldn't see where he was treading and Mandy had to hold his arm to guide him across. He walked forward hesitantly, putting one foot in front of the other slowly to feel for the stepping-stones. Once, he slipped, his foot going with a splash into the rushing water. Mandy gasped, her heart in her mouth.

Mandy heard her father mutter something under his breath as he fought to regain his balance. Steady at last, he stumbled on across. Mandy was never so glad to feel her feet on dry ground once more.

They scrambled up the bank and walked quickly along to the stile. Mandy helped her father over.

At last they reached the Land-rover. Mandy opened the tail-gate and Mr Hope placed Charley gently inside.

Mandy climbed in with her. 'I'll stay in the back,' she said. Now that Charley had been found, Mandy didn't want to leave her side for a minute.

James and the other two dogs clambered into the front of the vehicle. Mr Hope drove slowly and carefully home.

'I'll phone Bleakfell Hall when we get back, if you like,' James offered. 'Tell them we've found her.'

'Thanks, James,' Mandy said gratefully. 'They'll be so pleased.' She held Charley's head in her lap. The dog looked up at her then licked her hand.

When they arrived at Animal Ark, Mr Hope took Charley directly into the surgery. Mandy held her head while her father bathed and dressed Charley's wounded leg and gave her an injection of antibiotics.

'Will she be all right, Dad?' Mandy asked anxiously.

'She'll be fine. The wound's not very deep, thank goodness.'

James went off to phone the Hall with the good news. 'Ben's pleased as anything,' he said, coming back into the surgery. 'He's going to tell the others.'

Mr Hope carried Charley into the kitchen. He put her down on the floor. Jess came over to lick the Labrador's face. Charley hobbled towards the fire and into Jess's basket

'Oh!' Mandy laughed. 'Sorry, Jess . . . it looks as if you've lost your bed.'

But Jess wouldn't have it. She climbed in and curled up beside Charley.

'Make her a bowl of warm milk and biscuits,' Mr Hope suggested. 'She can have some meat later on.'

Mandy warmed a saucepan of milk on the stove and poured it over a bowl of dog meal. She took it across to Charley. The Labrador lapped it up hungrily, licking the bowl clean in just a few seconds.

'That's better,' Mandy said, stroking Charley's head. 'Now try to get some rest. Come on,' she said to James. 'Let's leave them both to have a good sleep. They deserve it.'

Later that afternoon, after James had gone home, Charley had visitors. Mandy went to answer the knock at the door. Hammond Curtis stood there with Ben Burton and Antonia Kent. Behind them stood George Sims.

Mandy invited them through into the kitchen. George Sims crouched down beside the dog basket. Mandy was pleased when Charley wagged her tail at him. He patted her head awkwardly.

'I should tell you off,' he said gruffly. 'But I suppose it was my fault you ran away.' Charley sniffed the sleeve of his jacket. He patted her head again then stood up. 'Thanks, young lady,' he said. 'I'm very grateful.'

Mandy blushed. 'It's all right, Mr Sims,' she said. 'Jess did it, really.' Mr Sims patted Jess's head.

'The new trainer's arriving later today,' Ben

said. 'George is going to pick her up at the station before he leaves.'

Mr Hope came in from the garden. He shook hands with Mr Curtis and Ben. Antonia Kent offered her cheek to him for a kiss. Mandy almost giggled as her dad looked a bit flustered.

'How long will it be before Charley can work again?' Mr Curtis asked.

'Next week, I should think,' Mr Hope replied. 'She'll limp for a while, but not badly.'

'Can we leave her here for you to look after, Mandy?' Mr Curtis asked. 'The new trainer's coming today but I'd be happier if Charley stayed with you.' He winked at Mandy.

'Well . . .' Mr Hope's eyes twinkled as he looked at his daughter. 'I suppose it will be all right.'

Everyone laughed as Mandy threw her arms round her father's neck. Her heart brimmed with joy as she kissed him soundly on the cheek. She felt honoured to be trusted with a film star dog!

'We'll get on with the scenes she doesn't appear in,' Mr Curtis said, looking relieved. 'But as soon as she's better, it's back to work.'

Antonia Kent opened her handbag. She took out a black and white photograph of herself dressed in the white silk frock she wore in the murder mystery. She took a pen and quickly signed it.

'Here you are, darling.' She thrust the picture in front of Mandy. 'Have this for your dressing-table.'

'Oh!' Mandy said. 'It's great. Thank you, Miss Kent. My friends at school will be really envious.'

Mr Curtis clapped his hands. 'OK, everyone. Back to work.'

'Slave driver,' Antonia Kent said, giving Mandy a wink behind Mr Curtis's back.

Charley and Jess barked goodbye.

A little over a week later, Charley was ready to go back to work.

That afternoon, Mandy rushed out of school as fast as she could. She was in a terrible hurry. There were chores to do, English homework – and maths – and she had to make Charley look beautiful for her return to Bleakfell Hall.

'Hey, what's the rush?' James called as Mandy jumped on her bike and pedalled furiously away from the school gates.

'It's Charley's last day at Animal Ark,' Mandy called over her shoulder. Her schoolbag bumped on her back. 'I've got to get her ready. We're taking her back this evening.'

'Well, you could at least wait for me!' James yelled as Mandy got further and further away.

Mandy waited for him to catch up.

'She looks great,' Mandy said. 'Her leg's healed up beautifully.' She suddenly felt sad. 'Jess is going to miss her like anything.'

'She'll be going back home in a few weeks too,' James reminded her.

'I know,' Mandy said sadly. Animal Ark would seem really empty without Jess and Charley.

They pedalled the two miles to Welford in no time at all. James stopped by Mandy's gate.

'Good luck for tonight,' he said.

Mandy smiled. 'Thanks. I'll feel really upset taking her back,' she confessed.

'You can always borrow Blackie,' James said generously.

Mandy managed a cheerful smile. She squared her shoulders. It was no good moping around. There'd be lots of other animals who needed her help. 'Thanks, James,' she said warmly.

'See you tomorrow!' James waved and pedalled off down the lane.

Mandy left her bike by the shed and went into the kitchen. Charley got up from her place by the fire and came to greet her. Mandy threw her bag down and gave the dog a hug. She looked into the deep brown eyes.

'You look great, Charley. But it's back to work for you, I'm afraid.'

Charley barked.

Mandy looked round. 'Where's Jess?' Suddenly, she heard a strange noise from the broom cupboard. A kind of snuffling, then a tearing noise. Something fell with a clatter and all at once Jess appeared with a yellow duster in her mouth. She let it drop to the floor, put her front paw on it then started trying to tear it up.

Mandy burst out laughing. 'Oh, Jess, you are funny.' She picked Jess up and prised the duster away from her. She hugged her close. 'You're a real monkey.' Mandy suddenly noticed just how tubby the terrier was. She had been so busy looking after Charley during the week that she really hadn't paid much attention to Jess.

Mandy put Jess on the table and felt her tummy.

Underneath she was a bit swollen. Mandy frowned. She knew it was silly but it really looked as if Jess . . .

Just then Mrs Hope came into the kitchen.

'Mandy,' she said with a smile on her face. 'Betty's outside in the car. She's got a surprise for you.'

Mandy's heart leapt. A surprise . . . That could only mean one thing: the poodle. She quickly put Jess down on the floor and ran outside.

Betty stood beside her old station wagon. And beside Betty, on a brand new blue lead with a blue leather collar, stood Antonia, the poodle. She wagged her tail when she saw Mandy run out. Mandy bent to scoop the little dog up in her arms. Her eyes were bright and healthy, her coat soft and fluffy. She looked plump and well – a picture of health.

Mandy's throat was so full of happiness she couldn't speak.

'I thought you'd like to take her to Mrs Platt yourself,' Betty explained.

'Oh, I would.' Mandy, looked at her with shining eyes. Then she looked at her mother. 'Shall I ring her now, Mum? I've got time to go over before tea. I can groom Charley a bit later.'

'If you like, sweetheart.'

Mandy ran back inside. 'Jean, can you give me Mrs Platt's number?'

Jean thumbed through the card index and came up with Mrs Platt's telephone number.

'Thanks.' Mandy quickly dialled. After two rings she heard Mrs Platt's voice at the other end.

'Mrs Platt,' she said breathlessly. 'It's Mandy Hope.'

'Hello, Mandy.' Mrs Platt sounded pleased to hear her.

Mandy quickly explained about Antonia. She heard Mrs Platt draw in her breath.

'Oh, Mandy.' Mrs Platt's voice trembled a little. 'How lovely. Yes . . . please bring her over straight away.'

Mandy ran back outside. 'It's OK!' she cried. 'I can take her now. I won't be long, Mum.' She took the lead from Betty's hand. 'Thanks, Betty.'

Mandy felt really proud to be walking along with Antonia. She had helped to save the little dog's life and was taking her to a wonderful new home. It was a great feeling.

Antonia trotted meekly beside Mandy, as good as gold, all the way to Mrs Platt's bungalow. When they arrived, Mandy spied Mrs Platt watching eagerly from the window.

The door opened. Mrs Platt stood with a wide smile on her face.

'Come in, come in.' She wrung her hands in delight. Mandy felt her heart turn over as she handed Mrs Platt her new pet. Mrs Platt cradled the poodle's soft coat against her face. Then she held the dog away from her to get a better look.

'She's wonderful, Mandy! Thank you so much.' She hugged the dog to her again, then laughed as Antonia licked her face.

Mandy's throat ached. It was really great to see Mrs Platt so happy. 'Her name's Antonia,' she told her.

Antonia wagged her tail and licked Mrs Platt's nose.

'What a grand name! She's beautiful, Mandy.' Mrs Platt put Antonia down on the floor and gave Mandy a quick hug. 'I certainly won't be lonely any more,' she said, smiling. Then her smile broadened. She pointed. 'Well, bless me. Look at that!'

Antonia had jumped up on to Mrs Platt's fireside chair. 'Antonia!' Mandy chided.

'Well, who can blame her after all she's been through,' Mrs Platt said. 'Mind you, I don't think I'll fit very well into her basket!'

Mandy was still smiling as she said goodbye. Mrs Platt scooped Antonia off the chair and went with her to the door.

Mrs Platt kissed Mandy's cheek. 'Thank you again, Mandy. I'll never forget your kindness.' She and Antonia watched as Mandy went out of the gate. A little way down the road Mandy turned to wave. She didn't think she would ever forget the sight of Mrs Platt standing with Antonia tucked comfortably under her arm as if they had been friends for ever.

After tea, Mrs Hope drove Mandy and Charley up to Bleakfell Hall. Jess went along for the ride.

The new animal trainer greeted them at the back door. She was a young woman with short, red hair. She wore a pair of denim dungarees over a check shirt. A badge on the collar said 'Stop Animal Experiments'.

'Hi, I'm Sue.' She bent down. 'Hello, Charley, I'm so glad to meet you at last.' Charley wagged

her tail happily. Sue fondled Charley's neck and gave Jess a pat.

Mandy looked at her mum. She gave a sigh of relief. Charley would be OK now. She and Sue were already friends.

'Mrs Hope,' Sue said, 'one of the horses cut herself today. Would you take a look?'

'Yes, of course,' Mrs Hope said.

'Would you take Charley indoors for me, Mandy?' Sue asked.

'I'd love to.'

Mandy took Charley and Jess into the kitchen. She'd been dying to see Mr Baggins again. And the cats, of course – and everyone else.

Mr Baggins sat on his perch. The cats were asleep by the fire. Charley and Jess went straight into the pantry. When Mandy looked they were lying side by side on Charley's blanket. *I'm definitely not the only one who's going to miss Charley*, Mandy thought.

'*Right, everyone*,' said Mr Baggins. A noise like hands clapped together came from his throat.

Mandy couldn't help giggling. Mr Baggins sounded just like Hammond Curtis. She wondered what *he* thought about Mr Baggins's new saying.

'*In your places and two sugars,*' the parrot squawked.

Mandy ruffled the bright feathers. 'Been behaving yourself, Mr B?'

'No, he hasn't!' Ben Burton came through the door. Charley came out of the pantry to greet him. 'Charley! Great to see you, girl.' Charley licked his hand.

'I'm really going to miss Charley,' Mandy said.

Ben put his arm round her shoulders. 'She looks great, Mandy. You've all done a really good job. Hey, why not come up to see the filming tomorrow. Bring James if you like.'

'I'll ask Mum,' Mandy said, feeling more cheerful. 'But I'm sure it'll be OK.'

Mandy and Mrs Hope were driving back to Animal Ark when Mandy remembered she was going to ask about Jess.

'Mum . . .' She gazed at her mother thoughtfully. 'Is Jess . . . ?'

She noticed a twinkle in her mother's eye as she glanced at her.

'Is Jess what, Mandy?'

Mandy shifted in her seat. 'Is Jess by any chance . . . ?'

Mrs Hope laughed out loud. 'Come on, Mandy. Spit it out.'

'Is Jess . . . ?'

'Yes, Mandy,' Mrs Hope said, still laughing. 'Jess *is* going to have puppies!'

Ten

'I thought so!' Mandy shouted gleefully. 'Mum, why didn't you tell me?'

'We thought we'd keep it as a surprise. We might have known you'd spot she was getting more than just podgy.'

Mandy clasped her hands together. 'Mum, isn't it great? What's Auntie Mary going to say?'

Mrs Hope made a wry face. 'I don't know. I expect Tad is the father.'

Mandy laughed. 'I thought Jess was missing

him. I didn't know they were *such* good friends!'
She turned round to look at the little terrier
curled up on the back seat. 'Oh, Jess, you clever
thing!' She felt she could burst with excitement.
'When, Mum . . . when is she having them?'

'Now calm down, Mandy,' Mrs Hope said,
patting her daughter's knee. 'We're not quite
sure . . . pretty soon though.'

'We must get things ready,' Mandy said. 'She'll
need somewhere to have them. She likes the
broom cupboard, I found her tearing up—'

Mandy's mother laughed again. 'Mandy, hold
your horses. It won't be quite yet. Don't go turning
out the cupboard just yet.'

'But she'll need somewhere,' Mandy insisted.

'We'll find her somewhere, don't worry,' Mrs
Hope soothed.

Back at Animal Ark, Mandy skipped into the
surgery with Jess. Mr Hope was just clearing up
after the last patient.

'Dad, Mum's told me about Jess!'

Mr Hope smiled broadly. 'We thought you'd
probably guess.'

'I did. I just had so much to think about I kept
forgetting to ask. Oh, Dad, I'm so thrilled.' She

picked Jess up gently and patted her stomach. Then she hugged the terrier close. Charley didn't need her now but soon there would be lots of other dogs to look after. Tiny, gorgeous Jack Russell puppies. She just couldn't wait!

Next morning, Mr Hope dropped them off at Bleakfell Hall for the day, complete with picnic lunch.

Mandy couldn't wait to tell Ben the good news about Jess.

'Congratulations, Jess!' Ben said when he heard. 'Sue said Charley's been moping around a bit. I expect she's been missing her.'

They found Sue grooming Charley in the kitchen. Charley looked great – a beautiful shining coat, moist nose. Mandy felt proud to have been the one to help rescue her.

Mr Baggins greeted them with his usual squawk.

'Better leave Jess in here,' said Sue, lifting Charley down from the grooming table. 'Charley will need all her concentration this morning.'

'Stay here, Jess,' Mandy began. But Jess was already curled up by the fire, fast asleep.

Mandy took a couple of pieces of orange from

a saucer on the table.

'Come on, Mr Baggins,' she called. 'Time for work.' Mr Baggins flew on to her shoulder.

They filed along the passageway and into the big hall.

'You'd better be good today, Mr Baggins,' Mandy whispered.

'*Yeah, yeah,*' said Mr Baggins.

In the big hall, Mandy placed the parrot gently on his perch. Everyone was ready.

'Right, over here with Charley, please.' Mr Curtis stepped forward.

'You take her over.' Sue handed the lead to Mandy.

'*Right . . . take your places,*' said a voice.

Everyone started to move into their positions.

'Did I say move?' Mr Curtis shouted. His face looked red with annoyance. 'Everyone stay where they are.'

'*Right . . . take your places.*' His voice came again.

The actors and crew looked at one another. Mandy burst out laughing. 'It's Mr Baggins,' she spluttered. Beside her, James put his hand over his mouth to control his laughter. All the crew were laughing too – even the man with the dagger sticking out of his chest.

'*Right . . . take your cup of tea,*' Mr Baggins squawked suddenly.

Even Mr Curtis was laughing by now. He wiped his eyes and waved his hand in the air. 'That's enough, thank you, Mr Baggins. *I'll* give the orders if you don't mind!' He pushed his cap to the back of his head. 'Never work with children or animals!' he said, grinning.

Then filming began in earnest. Before they knew it, it was almost lunch-time. After thirty-six takes, they had finally got the stabbing scene right.

'How would you like to be stabbed thirty-six times?' James whispered.

Mandy nudged him. 'Shh!'

Mr Baggins had been unusually quiet. He sat on his perch, a piece of orange skin in his claw. Once he tucked his head under his wing and went to sleep. No one seemed to notice. Except Antonia Kent. She kept a wary eye on Mr Baggins, whatever he did.

'Could you take Charley back to the kitchen please, young lady?' Mr Curtis sat on the top of a stepladder, looking down. 'Come back and watch the rest of the day's shoot if you like.'

'I'd love to,' breathed Mandy. 'Thanks.'

She quickly took Charley back to the kitchen. 'Stay,' she commanded, pushing her inside the door and closing it firmly. She didn't want to miss anything. Sue had already gone off to groom the horses.

It was another hour before Mr Curtis shouted, 'OK, everyone, take a break. We're outside this afternoon, don't forget.'

Everyone breathed a sigh of relief.

'Come on,' James said. 'I'm starving. Let's have our picnic!'

In the kitchen, the dogs were nowhere to be seen. The pantry door was slightly ajar.

'I bet the dogs are in there.' Mandy pushed open the pantry door. She peeped in. Charley was sitting in one corner. She pricked up her ears and looked at Mandy. She whined softly. It was as if she was trying to tell Mandy something – something very important.

Then there was another small sound. A whine and a series of tiny squeaks. Mandy opened the door a little more and went inside. She stopped suddenly. Her mouth fell open.

For there beside Jess, on Charley's blanket, were four squirming bundles. Tiny puppies, their eyes closed tight. Two black and white, two brown and white. So small they would fit into Mandy's palm. Jess was trying to lick them all at once. She glanced up at Mandy. 'Look,' she seemed to be saying. 'Aren't I clever?'

Mandy's eyes felt as if they were popping out of her head. 'James . . . here – quick!'

Jess – with four tiny puppies. It was just too good to be true!

James pulled a face. 'Wow! Aren't they . . . um – funny.'

'They're not *funny*,' Mandy said, feeling indignant. 'They're gorgeous.'

'They'll look a bit better when they're dry,' James muttered.

'Shh,' Mandy said. 'Jess will be insulted if she hears you.'

'They're lovely, Jess,' James said quickly. 'Wonderful.'

Soon all the film crew knew about the puppies in the pantry.

'We'd better leave her now,' Mandy said when they had all taken a peep. 'When Dad comes back we'll ask him what we should do.'

Just as she spoke, she heard her father's Land-rover pull up in the yard.

She ran outside. 'Dad! Dad, guess what?'

Mr Hope got out of the car. 'What now?'

Mandy pulled his arm to drag him inside. 'Jess's had her puppies. In the pantry!'

'The pantry! Well, trust Jess. She always did like her food.'

Mr Hope came in to examine the pups. 'They're all fine,' he said. 'We don't want to upset Jess, so we'll leave them here for tonight, if that's OK?' he said to Sue. 'We'll collect them first thing tomorrow.'

Suddenly Jess wagged her tail furiously. There, peeping from behind Mr Hope's legs, was Charley. Jess whined and Charley pushed through into the pantry.

'I think Charley better stay out,' Mr Hope began.

Mandy touched his arm. 'No, Dad,' she whispered. 'Look!'

Charley was licking one of Jess's puppies.

Mandy stood watching, her hands on her hips. 'She's going to be their auntie,' she said.

Everyone laughed. Mr Hope gave his daughter a hug. 'Fancy having a film star for an auntie,' he said, a broad grin spreading across his face.

'We'll come back first thing,' Mr Hope reassured Mandy as they drove back to Animal Ark. 'Jess is in good hands for tonight.'

'In good paws you mean,' James piped up from the back seat.

The next day, the film crew were packing up when they arrived to collect Jess. The rest of the movie would be made at the studio.

'I shall really miss you all,' Mandy said to Ben, giving him a hug.

'If you change your mind about being a vet, Mandy,' Hammond Curtis came down the stairs, a suitcase in his hand, 'just give me a ring. I'll find you a job as an animal trainer.'

'Thanks, Mr Curtis,' Mandy said, shaking his hand. 'But I don't think I will.'

Sue walked in with Mr Baggins in a cage. Charley followed at her heels. Mandy poked her finger through the bars of Mr Baggins's cage. 'Now, you behave yourself, Mr Baggins.'

'*Two cups of sugar,*' Mr Baggins said, looking annoyed at being shut in.

Mandy bent to hug Charley, sad at having to say goodbye. ''Bye, Charley, I'll watch for you on TV.'

Jess was safely tucked in the back of the Land-rover with her pups. Mandy squared her shoulders as she watched Charley clamber into the Animal Stars van. Jess and her little family needed her now. Her job with Charley was over.

'Come on then, Dad,' she said. 'Let's get Jess and her babies home.'

Mandy turned to take one final look at Bleakfell Hall as they drove through the wrought iron gates and headed for home.

Ahead, the winding road led down to the village. Mandy felt full of anticipation. Four puppies to care for until Aunt Mary came home from Australia! And Jess, of course. What fun they were going to have.

She wound down the window and took a deep breath of sharp, clear air. She could see the village now, nestling peacefully among great stretches of moorland. The familiar church spire rose comfortingly from the bundle of houses and shops. She would feel really special, walking Jess and her four puppies across the village green for all to see. And when it was time for them to go back home Mandy knew there would be plenty of other animals needing her care. She grinned to herself. *Life,* she thought happily, *is absolutely great!*

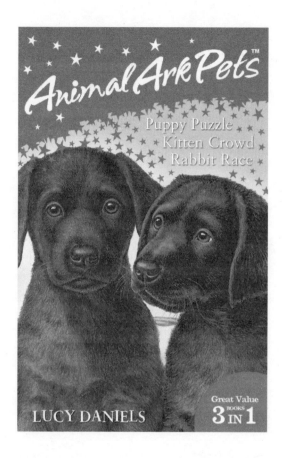

Three Animal Ark Pets books in one! In *Puppy Puzzle* two identical Labrador puppies are in a muddle! One of them has gone missing - but which one is it? Six newborn kittens are without a home in *Kitten Crowd* – can Mandy find them new owners by the end of the week? Whilst in *Rabbit Race* a baby rabbit is in danger, and only Mandy and James can help ...

For the full range of Animal Ark Pets
and Animal Ark books please visit

www.hodderchildrens.co.uk

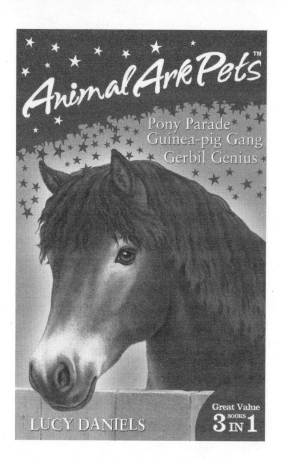

Paul's new pony is from a sanctuary, when people at school see it, they think he's been mistreating his pet. Can Mandy prove them wrong in *Pony Parade*? In *Guinea-pig Gang* Mandy has lots of friends with guinea-pigs and together they form a gang. But Lisa won't join in with her pedigree guinea-pig. Why is she being so snooty? In the exciting adventure *Gerbil Genius* Mandy and James find an escaped gerbil out in the wild. Can they tame him and get him used to humans again?

For the full range of Animal Ark Pets
and Animal Ark books please visit

www.hodderchildrens.co.uk